The Age of Fibs

Beth Spencer

stories memoir microlit
new & selected

ES-PRESS is an imprint of
SPINELESS WONDERS
PO Box 220
Strawberry Hills
NSW Australia 2012

shortaustralianstories.com.au

A short version of this book won the Carmel Bird Digital Literary Award and was first published as an ebook by Spineless Wonders in 2018.

This expanded version first published by ES-Press, an imprint of Spineless Wonders, 2022

Typeset in Garamond
Printed by Ingram Spark

ISBN 978-1-925052-38-1 (pbk)

Proudly supported by

A catalogue record for this book is available from the National Library of Australia

Distrust everything I say.
I am telling the truth.
— *Ursula K. Le Guin*

The dream deceives; it leads
to confusions; it is illusory.
But it is not erroneous.
— *Michel Foucault*

It's a poor sort of memory
that only works backwards.
— *Alice in Wonderland*

Contents

Bewitching

Six o'clock is the witching hour. Samantha, flying in on her broomstick, burning the dinner, transforming into a black cat, leaping into What's-His-Name's arms.

I lie on the green carpet, transfixed by the television, pretending I can't hear my mother as she calls and calls from the kitchen.

'Girls! Come set the table for dinner.'

Who would believe that Sam, who can conjure anything at the twitch of her lovely nose, would willingly trade wizardry for a kitchen whizz?

(This was the fantasy part.)

Ever-loyal helpmeet to Derwood as he casts his dreary capitalist spells, manipulating desire and peddling illusion. (No prizes for guessing who's the real creative genius.)

So many contortions and tricks necessary to allow the man of the house to believe he's the head.

The laugh track—*hahahahaha.*

But I didn't miss the way Sam keeps coming down with mysterious ailments. Like that morning she finds the doors and windows all sealed against her. (Trapped in the house.)

Or the time everything she touches turns gold. (A gilt complex!)

And the day whenever she sneezes a bicycle or tricycle appears.

'It's totally logical,' announces Doctor Bombay. 'In fact, it's cycle-logical!'

Dr Bombay twirls his moustache and diagnoses the problem: Sam has been suppressing her powers.

The solution: Simple. Start using them!

I curl on the Fler lounge biting my fingernails. Noticing how Sam flinches at Darrin's anger, his constant criticism whenever anything goes a tiny bit wrong (Julius Caesar in the kitchen, for instance, instead of a Caesar Salad).

That hint of violence under the laugh track.

But what do you expect if you agree to give up your powers?

To the other witches Sam is a fallen woman, a drudge to a man.

Meanwhile, here's Serena—Super fun gerroovay! Dark Lady to Sam's Fair Maiden.

'Fly me to the moon,' croons one of Serena's lovers, and next minute there he is up among the stars, bewildered.

Another one gets turned into a bedwarmer when she tires of him.

Everything so literal and full of puns—like dreams.

With Endora perched on the stairs, the mother-in-law of all jokes come home to roost.

For half an hour every weeknight I am part of a coven, exploring my Wiccan heritage. This quicksilver world where the galaxy is one's backyard, and where men can be a part of it but the feminine rules supreme.

The feminine, the queer, the magical—the irruption of the repressed right here into my living room every night at six o'clock.

Busting open all the doors and all the windows. Letting in the stars.

Fatal Attraction in Newtown

In a world not far away / thirty years ago / yesterday

1 THE PLAGUE YEARS

I love matinees. I avoid Saturday nights, because it's always couples. I prefer daytime, midweek: playing solitaire with the old, the homely, the chip rustlers and furtive chocolate eaters, the hanky-bringers.

We space ourselves out in the cavernous interior, settling back in the velvet seats. Wrap our arms around ourselves— like Alex in *Fatal Attraction,* shivering in the cold outside the Gallagher's warm bright country house.

In the village, miles away from New York, it was safe for them to stake your heart.

Everyone agreed you were a witch. You didn't belong.

In the Village Cinema they cheered when the bullet went in.

A man has unsafe sex while his wife's away and a woman dies, what's new? They were calling it the AIDS movie. It was 1987. The end of the weekend fling.

A dark plague-ridden world, illuminated by soft glowing hearth-fires through leadlight windows …

I was a couple once. Floating around the room joined at the hip. So engrossed in the steps. Not knowing where one body ended and the other's began, but so conscious of all those points of contact (fingers, back, elbow, hand, shoulder, oops—foot). I liked the way you'd sometimes bump into another couple, look across, smile, apologise …

Complicity. Dancing the world into circles.
(Alex on the outside, trying to get in.)
You went at each other like animals.

Water

taps

mirror

steam

mist

knife (*Alex*).

Poor Dan.

Alex keeps phoning him, tells him she's pregnant; he breaks into her flat, looking through her private things.

She lies to get into his house, meet his wife and get their phone number; he goes to her flat and assaults her.

She breaks into his house while he's away and kills their pet rabbit; he bashes her.

She goes completely mad and attacks his wife with a carving knife; he chokes her, pushes her under the water. She is still alive, rises up again; his wife shoots her dead.

Oh God, *poor* Dan …

I was in here, because I'd just been thrown out of court. Landing with a thud and a cra-a-ckk on the pavement, a million pieces.

I needed somewhere warm and dark to hide; so I came here, to plug myself into that great collective-unconscious of the cinema, to be embraced.

Alex: 'All the interesting guys are always married'—passing him food in her loft apartment, listening to his boring stories after having walked his dog.

'Well maybe that's why you find them interesting,' Dan says, 'Because you can't have them.'

She is already devoted, bitter, bitten, obsessed—why can't he see this?

Later, Dan: 'I thought we could have a good time.'

Alex: 'No you didn't, you thought *you* could have a good time, you didn't stop for a *second* to think about me.'

True. But she's a total maniac in this scene, so we side with Dan and his urge to get away.

When I told friends I'd been called up for jury duty they were envious: 'Aren't you lucky.'

I lay awake all night.

Alex's loft: the white virginal clothes, the white bed sheets and white walls; the lonely exercise bike in the corner.

No. 5 Court was small and low-ceilinged; not plush like the movies but with wigs and black capes, nonetheless. Those of us seeking exemptions were ushered to one side.

Shirking your duty was considered a crime. Flimsy excuses were given short shrift (sarcasm, humiliation, refusal). The early camaraderie of the exemptions section quickly gave way to a thick, heavy dread, like gravy.

Light and whiteness, showing up the blood so well when she does her knife trick to get his attention …

Almost everyone swore on the Bible. Occasionally someone would ask to take an affirmation and the judge would look up from his papers and peer silently at them over his glasses.

When my turn came I took a deep breath. 'I'm sorry,' I said, 'but I've thought about this long and hard. I've been an anarchist for ten years, and I just don't feel I can sit in judgement on another person.'

Gave herself a few gashes to show how she felt: a slit here, a slit there …

The gravy froze.

… Got her hands covered in blood; rubbed Dan's face in it.

A pin dropped somewhere near the back. No one moved. It was as if I'd opened my fist to reveal a small time bomb.

Then the judge turned puce and exploded, spluttering questions at me in an outraged voice. (I closed my palm, quickly.)

'Do you *know* what an anarchist *is?*'

He rolled the words around and spat them out, poking at them as if they were rodents. I reminded him I'd been one for ten years.

'An anarchist,' he boomed, 'is someone who wants *anarchy* in SOCIETY!'

(Well, hard to argue with *that*.)

Dan forces Alex to the sink, binds her wrists together with cloth. Men hate that (blood). Can't forgive being reminded.

'An anarchist is someone who wants decentralised decision-making structures …' I began, but he cut me off.

'If *you* committed a crime,' he paused for a moment, his tone suggesting I probably committed at least five a day, 'wouldn't *you* want to be tried by a jury?'

I said I wouldn't have a choice.

He spluttered and turned even more red (outraged!) and said, 'Get out of my *sight*, out of my court.' And in a voice full of disgust and loathing, 'I wouldn't even *inflict* you on the defendant.'

Your logic: thin, sharp, pointed and dangerous. You kept missing and cutting yourself. Even the weather and the music turned against you.

As I left the box there was a nervous rustling in the aisle seats. A woman tucked her skirt in, another edged a briefcase closer in beside her legs. My knees felt wobbly.

At the door, I tried to turn the shiny handle but I couldn't work out which way it went and fumbled hopelessly until after what seemed minutes a man sitting nearby leant across and gently opened it. I felt pathetically grateful because he dared to almost touch my hand when the judge had just said what a piece of scum I was. He even half smiled.

Dan says: 'That's crazy. You knew the rules.'
Alex says: 'What rules?'

Outside in the hallway, I waited for the elevator, and when it came I heard someone speeding up to catch it so I held the door. It was one of the women I'd been chatting to earlier in the exemptions corner. She stopped dead when she saw me. Took a step back. I held the door. Eventually she got in, standing as far away from me as she could, staring rigidly up at the numbers.

I said, 'The judge was rather severe, wasn't he?'

'Oh, they *have* to be,' she said. And then she assured me that she had a good respectable reason for not serving but would certainly be doing her duty *next* time.

Alex: in bed now, white and clean, neatly bandaged. All the blood safely locked back up into her skin, a pale heroine.

She hears him lie into the phone and whisper 'I love you' to his wife.

I went out into the street, it was eleven a.m., and I felt like a piece of shit.

So I came here to lose myself in the movies.

There are twelve of us, I've counted. We sit in the dark eating chocolate peanuts and crackling chip papers, watching and feeling the contact of our bodies soft against the seats.

Alex opens the door to Dan wearing a sexy teddy—after having invaded his inner sanctum and lied to his wife to get his phone number.

Someone in the dark behind me says, 'Ugh,' loudly, and there is a ripple of agreement.

Alex is a parody, a poor imitation. So unlike Dan, Beth and little Ellen at the start of the film, safe and vulnerable together in their sensible cotton underwear. Real intimacy.

What reviewers said about *How to Conceive of a Girl*:

If you immerse yourself and let the fragments accumulate, you get a new perspective on the messy, lateral workings of the human heart and mind. It's exhilarating. — Jenny Pausacker, *The Age*

A witty and engaging debut ... Beth Spencer takes the short story into new and unexpected directions. — Susan Johnson, Steele Rudd Award, judges report

Spencer writes with great verve ... *How to Conceive of a Girl* is an empowering, witty and incisive comment on the seventies and eighties sexual-cultural scene. — Thuy On, *Overland*

Writing that defies easy definition ... Spencer moves from dreamlike fantasy to acute analysis of sexual politics, mixing skewer-sharp character detail with luridly funny evocations of the 70s, juxtaposing pop-culture savvy with searching evocations of desire. Rewarding and engrossing reading. — Phillipa Hawker, *Marie Claire*

Spencer's book will appeal to anyone with an interest in ways of breaking out of sequential narrative. Her montage or collage assembly of incidents and reflections ... attract me enormously ... the playfulness of the methods and the self-questioning throughout reflect an intellectual toughness that deserves to be encouraged and promoted. — Michael Sharkey, *The Weekend Australian*

Spencer's stories ... made me laugh, they constantly made me reflect, once or twice they made me cry. A talented and inspiring writer. — Enza Gandolfo, *Australian Women's Book Review*

Beth Spencer has developed a mode of narrative which seems effortlessly to embody complex and intensely mobile ideas. Everything dances. — Peter Bishop, former Director Varuna Writers Centre

Witty, emotionally powerful, and very crisp. — *Arts Today*, ABC-RN

Quirky imagery and delicious fragments … and a tempting title that suggests a sort of postmodern portraiture, or a subversion of discourses about defining the feminine. The book is marketed as a collection of short stories, but this does not do justice to the structure, the intertextuality, and the finely woven fabric of the text. — Felicity Plunkett, *Antipodes*

Spencer is not a writer to cast you a linear life-line. But as she says of writing about the 70s: 'Maybe realism is inadequate for exploring the confused contradictory fragmented mess that it was'. So go with the flow when reading this. One connection invariably leads to another and, despite the jagged edges, the prose glides. — *The Herald Sun*

As relevant today as it was when it was first published, if not more so. Highly recommended. — Kim Kelly

I've been re-reading Beth Spencer's brilliant collection, *How to Conceive of a Girl*. I got my copy almost 20 years ago in Australia. I just love the book. It's before its time. — Elizabeth McCracken, finalist National Book Award

By revealing that there's nothing 'natural' about being / becoming / conceiving of a girl, by bringing this into language, literature and therefore culture, Spencer makes it more possible to rethink / renegotiate the social contract … There are dangers involved in broadening gender definitions, in boundary crossing, in abseiling and hang-gliding from secure subject positions; in bringing the unknown, the unarticulated, the disavowed into cultural consciousness. It's a serious business … and I'm always grateful and amazed, renewed in my attempts to continue doing this when I read work like *How to Conceive of a Girl.* You could say that it en/genders courage. — Kathleen Mary Fallon, *ABR*

Beth Spencer flings herself into textual free-fall in this strange, delightful book. The collection simply buzzes … More please. — *The Good Weekend*

What reviewers said about *Vagabondage*:

Searingly honest and sometimes darkly funny. — Andy Jackson, *Australian Poetry Journal*

I'd like to nominate Beth Spencer's *Vagabondage* as my best read for 2014 … It's beautiful, it's funny, it's sad, and it speaks to all of us who aim to age disgracefully. — Suzanne Donisthorpe, *Books & Arts Daily*, ABC-RN

Beth Spencer has a great eye and ear for detail, for small things with larger implications … A book to read and re-read, and re-inhabit. — Phillipa Hawker

There are authors for whom writing functions as a form of truth-telling … We look to them for insight and intelligence and good humour, and a willingness to share—and Beth Spencer is one of them. *Vagabondage* is a short work that leaves you feeling you've read a much longer one. There are many reasons for this, not least her close-focused but at the same time expansive and warm angle on the universe. — Angelo Loukakis, *Rochford Street Press*

Each poem builds up to a memoir of deep self-reflection on what it means to be alive on this earth. Mingling lighthearted observation with deep, warm and above all intimate introspection that the reader is invited to join, so that the journey becomes a shared one between the poet and the reader. — Magdalena Ball, *Compulsive Reader*

There is a humour that underlies the journey that turns its reading into an adventure … This book doesn't belabour its wisdom, but instead opens us up … to all aspects of humans' being. — Angela Gardner, *Cordite*

A joy to read … light as a breeze, and dark as a buried bone. — Jennifer Compton, Stillcraic

So much fun to read. Warm, witty and profound. — Claudia Taranto, ABC Radio National

Also by Beth Spencer

Things in a Glass Box (poetry)

How to Conceive of a Girl (fiction)

Body of Words (double audio CD)

Vagabondage (poetry memoir)

The Party of Life (poetry)

Never Too Late (poetry chapbook)

She makes us sick and angry.

I tried to have sympathy with her, but there is so much violence in the film, and most of it is against her and it all seems so reasonable: I mean, if she is going to be so *un*reasonable.

Come on, Alex, just accept *reality*! (Dan's.)

Defence lawyer to alleged victim—now be reasonable, *dear. Surely you don't want to ruin a good man's life over this? Isn't there some more polite, less public way?*

Alex wanted to play by *her* rules, which said that if a man is happy with his wife then he doesn't fool around.

But the audience sides with Dan. *She's not playing by the rules* (the ones that make it safe for men), *she's ruining it for everyone.*

She wanted to be Madame Butterfly but she was Madame Reptile, slithering along the floor, with Dan chasing her down the hallway, throwing her against the wall, grabbing her legs *(a pregnant demented thing, a witch, a bloated repulsive evil …)*

She wants respect, but look at her, running after him, begging and pleading.

Dan with his sarcastic lawyer's tongue and impeccable logic, battering her up against the wall …

'You tell my wife and I'll kill you.'

'Kill her now, Dan,' a woman in the audience says, thumping the edge of the seat in front of her gently with her fist.

Alex says: 'I *love* you, Dan … Why are you so hostile? I'm not your enemy.'

Dan's anger, so logical; Alex's, so hideous and terrifying. Dan says: 'It's *over*, Alex.' An incantation.

She is repulsive, but the rejected and abandoned become that way, no one wants the stink of failure.

(The man in court today, leaning across to open the door: *thank you*.)

She is a clinging vine. Spotted the cracks, the flaws in his family life, chiselled her way into the hairline fractures and split them apart. Gate-crashed his defences: got past his secretary, deceived her way into his house. Dan is foiled by politeness, forced to be a gentleman in public; it was his Achilles heel and she took it in her mouth and bit, hard.

And when she shakes his hand her thumbnail is red, like a bird of prey.

I ease open my peanuts slowly; the cellophane crackles and the woman in front looks accusingly over her shoulder at me.

'I *love* you, Dan.'

She circles his house in the country with its warm hearth fire and happy glowing faces. Hugs herself in the cold. Vomits in the bushes. Moves in for another bite.

Evidence, your honour: what normal woman would grow sick at the sight of a happy healthy family?

She throws herself in his face. Etches her initials on his family Volvo with acid.

My lord, my lord, a pregnant, abandoned and frightened one might.

Terror tactics: forcing Dan to tell more lies.

(Poor Dan.)

Alex: 'I'm not going to be *ignored*, Dan.'

And then she boils the pet bunny rabbit in the family cooking pot.

It is as if the air-conditioner has malfunctioned. All the breath suddenly sucked out of the cinema. Ellen's scream inside my chest.

'You *bitch*,' the woman behind me hisses, a long slow exhalation. It moves softly over the backs of the seats in a wave, connecting up our anger like a current, a thin taut wire.

Once there were two men, Dan and his friend Jack, and they created the ultimate sexy fantasy woman—sensual, energetic, full-blooded, abandoned, wild, independent, even intelligent. Dan had sex with her and afterwards when he went to put her back in her box, she said *no*. Inch by inch the dream (male porno movie) turned into a nightmare (horror flick).

She became possessive, clingy, demanding, pregnant.

(Mad.)

Dan in his Volvo.

Alex following him obsessively in a red car.

Alex's voice on the cassette tape: '*This is what you've reduced me to.* Part of you is growing inside of me, Dan. I feel you, I taste you, I think you, I touch you. I bet you don't even like girls, do you? Fucking faggot!'

We close in around Beth and Dan, and cute little Ellen, forming a protective circle.

A woman gets an emotional stranglehold on a man and so he gets a real one on her: an old story. (Watch out, Alex!)

There are two sides to every coin and Alex is the dark one, the swept under the carpet side—the nuclear family flipped out.

In the bathroom: barefoot and pregnant.

Alex's face behind Beth's face in the misty mirror.

Standing there with her twisting knife. (*So difficult to kill with your double life.*) Slashing at the skin of her thigh like a madwoman, talking calm like a lawyer. The room steaming up, the bath overflowing, the blood collecting in a pool at her bare white feet. (*Had your Salem witch dress on.*)

Blood

water

salt

saliva

sperm.

Leaky fluids, seeping through the ceiling into the clean kitchen below.

'Quick, Dan! *Now!*' someone shouts.

Your honour, my client held her under the water and strangled her till she stopped breathing purely in self-defence. *And when she rose up still alive, there was* no choice *but to shoot her in the heart.*

After all, a man's home is his castle.

The audience trembled in the dark while Dan grabbed her by the neck and choked and pushed her under the water. (*Drowning, just the test.*) You could see the light flickering on the faces of those closest to the front.

Stone her, burn her at the stake, drive a nail through her heart!

When she rose up out of the water we screamed, and when the bullet went in (the final solution) some people cheered. The blood streaming out of her like a thick black stake, nailing her to the wall, arms outstretched …

I stayed till the very end, till after the ambulance took the body away and the calm ambient music returned and the last slow zoom shot of the happy family photo in the hallway.

*

I guess I wasn't surprised to see Alex (Glenn Close) in the cinema powder room—white tiles, mirrors, taps—after all, a bathroom was where I'd seen her just a few minutes before.

In the powder room she looked like anyone else. Her curly hair tight and ordinary now, more like her character in *The Big Chill* (Artemis, the Earth Mother).

She had on a fawn wool wraparound coat and tan stockings and a big black leather bag on a strap and she was leaning over the basin, splashing cold water onto her face.

When I came out of the cubicle she was gone.

2   A CLOSE ENCOUNTER

I saw her again a week later on the Newtown 423 bus.

I noticed because of the Medusa hair, those wispy blonde curls all over her head, little helixes and corkscrews. I'd been reading about it in the library.

She was sitting next to a man whose smell of garlic was overpowering, like a safety shield, and she was craning her neck to see past him out the window, with that desperate look of someone who might have missed their stop.

Mosquitoes May Spread AIDS a headline screamed. The boy next to me was reading an article on domestic violence.

It was funny because when I got on the bus there were two girls near the door and one said, 'Speak of the devil.' And then I went and sat down the back and there she was, in her fawn wraparound coat. So close I could touch her. I put my hand on the back of the seat, and let my knuckles graze the edge of her collar.

Medusa was death, I knew that. To see her face to face was to die. She was also the present and the future; the destroying aspect of the triple Goddess, with magic blood that could create and destroy life.

I knew more about Alex this time, too (I'd been reading an article in the library). I knew that the director tried to let her escape with an off-screen suicide, but the preview audiences demanded a violent ending. They wanted to see her die horribly (held under with her legs jerking like a shock-treatment victim). They wanted a thorough scourging, to see the bullet and the warm stream of blood.

Up on a billboard, far above the cars, a woman is being sawn in half.

I have a house in Newtown at the bottom of the street, where all the debris washes down and collects in a big pile. I have passionflowers growing over the back fence, and blackberries, and arum lilies in the front garden.

If Alex had come to visit I would have said, 'Forget him, he's trouble; you're worth more than that creep, he'll drive you mad.'

In my report I would say that Alex needs to be referred to a therapist and Dan should do community service.

But the audience said, *No. Burn her at the stake!*

I lean forward, pretending to tie my shoelace, to see if you are still pregnant, but it's impossible to tell. There are raindrops on the window. At Sydney University a new batch of passengers come in. They pirouette, dripping wet coats onto our laps, furling umbrellas in damp pointed bundles that poke up under our skirts and between our knees, into the folds of our shoes.

That's when I notice Dan (Michael Douglas) up the front, sitting in the seat reserved for old or lame people. I watch the back of his head, until he turns it slowly and looks down towards us. I try to see your reaction but you don't even notice—too busy looking out of the window. Or perhaps you haven't met him yet?

(I can feel the electricity from your hair on my fingertips.) Dan sees me watching him and turns back calmly to face the front.

And then I spot Beth (Anne Archer) about halfway down on the opposite side. She's reading a paperback with a pink cover and has a round cane shopping basket on her knee.

Friday night rush. The bus belches along and the man with the garlic gets up, breathing heavily. The boy closes his newspaper and punches the button for the next stop.

Suddenly I feel frightened and I rest both of my hands on the bar of the seat in front of me, close my eyes and try to beam a message: Stay away from married men, and keep away from the suburbs!

It's my stop. I push past the people in the aisle, letting my hand touch her sleeve as I pass. (I don't believe their story, I think you've been framed.)

I glance quickly down at her wrists but the coat sleeves cover them; there are bandaids over the slash marks on her thigh. (You've been cutting yourself again, haven't you?)

The bus starts to lurch forward but someone yells out 'Door!' and then I am outside. The chill air.

Wind
leaves
creaking buildings
holes in the pavement
rubbish skips.

In the window of the Op Shop: baby clothes, a stuffed pink rabbit, cooking pots, a set of knives, knitting needles, bobby pins, homemade pottery vases with decayed dried flowers, a jumble of earrings and false eyelashes and Isadora Duncan-style scarves, tea towels with crocheted hooks to hang them on the wall.

The doormat says 'Welcome'.

At the entrance to the hydroponics shop a 'Feed ME!' plant flaps its leaves angrily and a man wheels a little 'feed me' monster around the corner towards me, its red round mouth open wide with that little dangling thing in the back of its throat wagging. I step out of the way and they hurry past.

And then something attacks my shoulder, pecking with a hard jabbing motion. I whirl about and grab it as it attempts to fly off. (My aikido training: accept the incoming force, embrace it to you and make it a part of yourself. Bring it into line with your own body so you can direct its energy.)

It's a hand. Yours.

Night fills in all the pockets of the street in quick black flakes, and I am back in the cinema: your almost-translucent skin. Those wispy curls all over your head, like a halo.

You look startled and I squeeze your hand reassuringly. (Your skin is so warm.)

I laugh when you ask the way to Watkins Street. (Glenn Close asking directions!) I know I sound like a maniac, but what do you expect? You're so famous.

I point the way and there's a pause. As if one of us has forgotten her lines, and then I realise you're waiting for me to give back your hand. (A nice hand.)

I let go and you retrieve it absently, as if it's a glove, and place it on the top of your bag. And then I turn and walk off in the opposite direction because I've just directed you to my street, and I'm embarrassed that you might think I'm following you. At the entrance to Bucknell Street I turn for a moment and you're still standing there, staring at your body reflected in the black marble of the funeral parlour.

People collect into little eddies around you and circle past.

I think about the piece of paper in your hand. Whose address? What rendezvous are you hurrying to meet?

In my house at the end of the street I provide refuge for the unreasonable. Ophelia, Madame Butterfly, Rochester's mad wife from *Jane Eyre*: the discarded ones, the drowned women, the self-mutilators.

The pieces of dog shit: like Alex, stuck on Dan's shoe making him so angry and irritated because it was so persistent.

(Dan stepped on a crack, and a little chink of concrete fell away, and a black silent smoke began to escape and it followed him home because it recognised him as its master.)

Newtown has become dangerous: every second house blinks at me with a tiny red eye.

And suddenly I remember Beth and Dan. In the crush at the end I didn't notice if they stayed on the bus.

I hear footsteps and turn quickly. A shadow melts into a side street.

3   STREET SEX

Promiscuity: making love in elevators

One night I was stepping out, and a man was walking towards me, on his way somewhere like I was on my way home. And instead of looking past each other like you do in elevators and streets, we held each other's gaze.

Like a caress. A long slow sensuous dance along King Street. We put our whole bodies into it. Held back nothing.

He was a perfect stranger, and for that moment we made love as if there was nobody else in the world more important. It lasted for perhaps a minute (forever). And then we passed each other in the dark.

'Hey,' he cried.

I looked back and shook my head.

There is a purity about a one-night stand when you accept the total stranger-ness of the other. When you have no thought of whether 'something will come of this' and are just making love because this is a fellow human being; rather than making love because you want love back.

Alex wanted love back, wanted it desperately. (*Pulled back the elevator grille like a jailer.*) She wanted respect from Dan because she didn't know if she deserved it.

And if she couldn't have Dan then she wanted to be beautiful tragic Madame Butterfly but they made her into the Mosquito Woman instead.

*

A man with a tie and a man with a bike

One evening, riding on the back of a friend's motorbike we passed first a man in a black suit and white shirt, then a young woman carrying two bags of shopping.

'That man's following that woman,' my friend said. He'd seen the man hanging around outside the shopping mall, checking people out.

'Stop!' I said.

He pulled up and I ran across the road and waited at the lights until the woman came level and then I stopped her and asked her to glance back and see if she knew the man. She didn't.

I suggested we cross the road.

She was like the night, warm and open; trusting, but I had frightened her.

We pressed the pedestrian button and meanwhile the man slowed his pace. When he got closer he loitered, looking in an empty shop window. The woman and I pretended to be old friends, chatting. When the lights changed we crossed the road, and I looked back and watched the man hesitate, then turn around and go down a side street.

The thing was that my friend had noticed that the man was wearing a tie when he left the shopping mall. But by the time we caught up with him at the lights, he wasn't.

*

Slips and spillages

The man and the bike and I had an accident once. Skidding suddenly across the road on our sides, with traffic stopped all around us. Spotlights, centre stage. Lights being picked up and made into thick rainbow colours in the oily asphalt. I was pillion and my helmet kept bouncing on the road. We only had one between us and had just spent ten minutes arguing who should wear it. I lost, and now, lying almost on my side, I watched the beautiful bare head of the man I loved an inch in front of me, feeling my own bounce on the asphalt and waiting for his to explode like a peach in my arms. But he held his head up and turned around to look at me while we still danced sideways. 'Are you alright? Are you alright?' we both kept saying: making love with our bodies and eyes, feeling the night air on our skin, in touch, in front of all those people in their safe steel and plastic enclosures.

You can move so much more quickly on a bike and avoid danger, but if you do fall, then there is nothing to catch you.

Bike sex
road sex
street sex
elevator sex
kitchen sex
bedroom sex
bathroom sex
sex-sex.

*

Fly-sex

Once, long ago, I saw two flies having sex. Blowflies. It went on for ages. Gripped together, the male fly on top, riding the female fly who staggered about buzzing and groggy. Sometimes she tried to fly away a bit but he clung on. Or maybe it was him that flew, carrying her underneath? It went on for such a long time. I got bored.

Irritated. In the end I picked up a brick and dropped it on them.

4   VAMPYRE HUNT

You could see Beth's face in the mirror and you could see Alex's, but did you notice that we never once saw Dan's reflection?

Night was closing in around me, a thick cape.

Somewhere down in South Newtown a police chase was on, and a belt of backyard dogs began joining in.

In our house at the end of the street, beautiful Antoinette (the one Rochester has named Bertha) plays out Jane's wedding fears with her white veil and the candles and the mirror. She dances down the stairs, around the lounge-room, and out again.

In my room at the front I sleep in a big double bed like a boat. I have this recurring nightmare that I am walking down the aisle in Antoinette's long white dress, with my father beside me.

I can't imagine how I have agreed to this. I stare at the bouquet of trailing frangipani in my hands, at the guests. They smile at me, I see their faces white and misty through the veil, I can't breathe …

And then Alex walks in; she hands me a knife.

*

The bunny girl: a small story

Once there was a little girl next door who had a bunny. The bunny bit the girl savagely on the hand and ran away. So the little girl let the bunny live under the neighbour's house but claimed her back whenever she wanted a possession to show off to visitors (rare). She has no friends. The little girl is lonely, she will grow up to be Alex. Her name is Ellen.

Even bunnies reject her.

*

Dan's life is a menagerie: bunnies, snakes …

Bunnies have phantom pregnancies if they don't have a mate. Lumps grow inside them instead of the real babies they crave and become cancers that eventually kill them.

Bunnies circle the one they love—their human 'owner' if there's no real bunny around—coming in closer and closer each time, staring at you with their mad pink eyes.

… Like Nell Bowen in the movie *Bedlam*: 'I'm not mad! I'm *not* mad!' Sounding crazier by the minute.

(Run, Ellen, quick!)

*

In my house at the end of the street we will need at least six phone lines as we all sit about waiting for phone calls that never come.

Bars on the windows. Triple locks on the doors. It's dangerous in here.

You were so mad, so edgy.

Of course Dan was originally 'tender' and said, 'Sorry Baby', and stuff like that but he never once talked to Alex like a real human being with a real problem. He was full of lines, they spun out of his mouth, hooked under her tongue.

Alex said: 'Call me sometime? You don't have to if you don't want to.'

Dan: 'No, I want to, I really do.'

(Lies.)

His violence: always so logical.

Remember the rules, Alex. You *knew* the rules, Dan says you did. The rules of Adult Entertainment. (You know, those movies where women get tied up and fucked.)

I quickened my pace. At Bucknell Lane I glanced down towards Watkins Street and saw Alex hurrying past in her fawn coat.

Alex has Dan's life inside her now, a small voodoo doll, tucked under the folds of her belly. She has control over it, life and death. Dan wants it back.

Wind
rubbish
blood.

In the bathroom: so difficult …

Blood and water—a birth scene, and a resurrection scene rising out of the waves like a true Goddess with your Medusa hair. A *Psycho* scene, but who were the psychos? After all, you were the one who got killed.

Alex is in the street parallel to me now, looking in the lighted windows.

Somewhere in the shadows behind her: Dan in his expensive grey coat, with the collar pulled up to keep out the wind.

Rubbish
blood
water
breath.

I turn quickly down a side lane and as I turn I catch a glimpse of a cane shopping basket disappearing behind a car.

Newtown bathrooms: so white, so clean. With stained-glass windows and deep claw-footed baths.

(Don't be afraid to empathise with Alex: we've all felt murderous, crazy, lonely, anti-social, rejected.)

But of course, Alex came on so *strong* …

Listen. Hear the distant clattering? The four horsemen. Tomorrow the council gardeners will shake their heads in dismay at the churned up circles on the grass.

Flies are such filthy disease-carrying things; rabbits are vermin.

(Dan's life: a menagerie.)

Dan is so sure that the rules are on his side that he asks a policeman. But the policeman says, actually, Sir, the rules aren't all on your side.

I decide to circle back around Wilson Street, to see if I can see what Beth is up to.

You went at each other like animals …

Alex with her nesting instinct.

Dan: frightened as a child for the suicidal Madame Butterfly; his father comforting him while he hid under a chair. ('She knew the rules, son.')

Someone is taking a shower. The light behind the misted window.

Poor Dan, so full of remorse. See him in the shower trying to soap it off. See how bad he feels having to lie again to his beloved wife. See how weak and indifferent he is when he keeps going back again for more.

Dan is the little boy who stole a cookie, he's only really remorseful because he broke the cookie jar in the process and got found out.

Messy Dan, didn't even offer to use condoms. Assumed he could ejaculate into you and like a good woman you'd clean it up (any mess: a foetus for instance).

But even Mills and Boon heroes know they have to use condoms these days.

Nothing is safe anymore, nothing is sacred. Sex is animal. You do it in elevators.

You do it on stairs like possums, like rabbits.

The roof is caving in—watch out! Careful of the baby's crib …

Under the frangipani tree, a man with a white shirt and a black suit (no tie) stands against the wall. A glint of steel. 'It's over,' an incantation.

I shake my head at the man on the bike.

We circle back.

If you have no one to dance with, you sit against the wall until your feet decay into mulch and little creepers sprout up the brickwork. Sickly flowers blossom behind your teeth, moon white, pale unhealthy green, hiding the evil thoughts that root in your heart and swell in your mouth.

Alex says: 'You play fair with me, and I'll play fair with you,' but there are no 'rules' for this.

In our house, Madame Butterfly folds her hands together and totters on crippled feet to the tap, while Antoinette parades around the living room, tearing up the furniture (will somebody please take that knife away from her before she cuts someone else!).

Nell Bowman looks in the mirror above the fireplace and whispers, 'I'm not mad!'

There is a click at the gate. His footsteps on the gravel. We dim the lights. One of the drowned women lights some candles, bites her fingernails (which are decaying anyway). The mirror is dark, just a patch—whose face is that in the background? Yours?

'Put the kettle on, Dan,' someone whispers. Antoinette darts up the stairs, leaving strips of lace caught on nails. In the corner Ophelia is giggling over a pink paperback book. Alex takes a knife and a piece of fruit from the cane shopping basket on the table.

The kitchen knife
the white sheets
the white rabbit
the cooking pot.

The kettle is already boiling, see it?
　'Come on in, Dan.'
　'We're waiting.'

Extinction Event

There are some who are in darkness
— Brecht

I was playing piano in a restaurant at the end of the world. Soup of the Day was Blue Tongue Lizard. The torch singer turns up the heat, mascara running down their face, scorching a song popular last century. You serve a Molotov and a Hemingway to a prickly customer. I'm itching to call the Bouncer. (Those talons in the wife's shoulder, not the strong silent type.) A party of rich punters, fingers fluid with jewels, applaud. A call goes up for Mack the Knife. The rumble of cutlery on linen. Then the stars go out. We knew this would happen. Try to tote up the bill in the dark. Split the difference! some say. Unfair! others cry. And on the ceiling, far up, a delicate chandelier hangs. Suspended, like black ice.

The Age of Fibs

Time for loving, time for caring,
time to move, yes it's time
— 1972 ALP campaign jingle

I must, I must, I must;
I must increase my bust!
— 70s schoolgirl chant

It was in 1971 that the Tech school I went to introduced Cookery and Needlework classes for the boys and, a year later, Woodwork and Sheetmetal for the girls. Although our form missed out on Woodwork because there was a shortage of trained teachers. We got Biology with Mrs Pivlovski instead.

Looking back, I don't remember anyone's parents (or any teachers or students) complaining about this. Maybe they did, and we just didn't hear about it. Or maybe it was incredibly gasp-radical for the first few weeks and then it just became incredibly normal. Like David Bowie wearing make-up, and Gary Glitter's platform shoes.

For the first few years these classes, unlike the less physical Maths and English, were always segregated. We liked having these all-girl classes, and we liked Sheetmetal, because Mr Harvey let us listen to the radio. Wednesday afternoons were passed happily watching Mr Harvey make anodised nut bowls and enamelled pendants while we perched in rows up on the benches, swinging our legs, brushing each other's hair, singing along to Suzi Quatro and the Kinks.

Music, taught to us by Mr Foster the Senior Master, was another 'physical' and hence segregated class. We had to sing a song and our class chose 'Nobody's Child' and sang it with great passion (*just like a flower ...*). Mr Foster, in his tweed suit, sat on the edge of the desk at the front of the room and said we were very sensitive; much more sensitive than the other class of girls in our year who had chosen to sing 'Dizzy.'

And then out of the blue he shocked us by talking about how opera singers always have such large bosoms.

No one said a word.

The thing was that if Mr Foster (who was at least forty) had noticed the bosoms of opera singers, then perhaps he had noticed ours (those of us who had a bosom).

And if *he'd* noticed (way too horrible to think about!), perhaps our fathers had too.

We knew the younger teachers had this area under surveillance after the famous case of Belinda Tilley who sprouted over the holidays (real breasts, firm and grapefruit-like, not the pointy embarrassing and painful things most of us began with). Mr Saunders commented on it at the sports carnival as she sped past round the track for the 200 metres, breasts streaking jauntily ahead in her new larger sized blue t-shirt.

'Jesus. How long has Belinda had tits?'

And at the other end of the scale, standing in a circle with us girls, talking, Mrs Kennedy, the cookery teacher, suddenly looks at me and says, 'Funny, I never realised you were flat, Angela.'

I wasn't sure whether I should feel insulted or vaguely complimented.

I mean, she did say she never realised.

And then that terrible time in Maths when the relief teacher (who no one liked anyway) mistook Berenice McKenzie for a boy.

'You there, young boy, what's the answer?'

Berenice's skirt was hidden by the desk and all that was visible was her round freckled face, short hair, and her straight as a board chest with the white shirt, school tie and blue jumper.

The room went ice-quiet. Berenice blushed deep beetroot and tears came to her eyes.

The relief teacher said, 'What's the matter? What's the matter?'

No one said a word. (Too slow, Mr Turcotte, go to the bottom of the class.)

And then, when he realised, he tried to make light of it, as if it didn't matter. Or as if it was Berenice's fault for tricking him by having short hair *and* a flat chest.

It was the boys I felt most sorry for though, when I heard about wet dreams.

Imagine just dreaming away about whatever it is boys of that age dream about (pet dogs? winning the 1500 metres? football?) and suddenly waking up in a pool of urine! Awful. Fancy having to tell your mother and having your mattress hung out the window to dry like a child.

I figured periods and bras were something that bonded you. ('Oh shit, I've got Fred,' and 'Bummer, poor you.') Whereas this terrible affliction that struck boys could surely only send them further and further into shame and isolation, lone wolves in their families, perpetually humiliated and exposed by their uncontrolled adolescent bodies. Never knowing when it might strike next.

Yes, boys certainly had it bad.

That thing about their dick changing to different shades of blue and purple just before their balls dropped didn't sound like it would be too much fun in the changing rooms either.

Meanwhile, I was having rather weird dreams myself. Dreams of having emotional-sexual experiences with bits of architecture: corners of the tiled roof, the delicate pattern around the ceiling, the architrave between two doors.

I would wake from these charged up, my body humming, and my mind awash in warm fuzzy sensations of perfect love. And then I'd remember that it was a piece of the house that I'd been so fondly (and sometimes indecently) engaged with and the perfect love feeling would spring a massive leak and ooze away.

Still, it was hard not to look forward to these dreams (you never knew when they would strike). And hard to look at the ceiling or the roof in quite the same way again.

Once I went and stood next to the architrave (a section of it that was a little similar to the dream one) and pressed the cotton socked toe of my foot against it gently to see if I could conjure up the feeling. But my brother suddenly burst in through the hall door and gave me such a look as he stormed past to his room that I felt instantly ashamed, and after that I made sure I walked by quickly, although I still felt a kind of bond.

It was the season for big changes all round. Not just Belinda Tilley, but out there in the wider world too.

The Australian Labor Party started the 'It's Time!' campaign and every night on the news there would be another one of those Labor devils—Gough Whitlam, Lionel Murphy, Bob Hawke, Jim Cairns, Al Grassby, Lance Barnard—spouting off about something and causing my father to rattle his spoon in his teacup and swear under his breath. ('You bar ... of soap, you!')

Actually, I thought the ads about the environment and equal pay and free education made a lot of sense, but then the Liberal's ad would come on, with a big black ball and chain and the ominous frightening words: 'Don't sentence yourself to 20 years hard Labor!'

If Labor got in, the ad said, they'd change the laws so that we'd never be able to get them out again. Hmm. Well, we couldn't let *that* happen.

Around this time a new women's magazine started up, called *Cleo*, edited by Ita Buttrose. It was the first ever Australian magazine run by a woman. Apparently, the preliminary market research said: 'Do not do this project, you will fail'. But they went ahead, and ran jaw-dropping articles about sex and orgasms, with nude centrefolds of famous actors, like Jack Thompson posing as Venus in a Titian painting, or the entire Skyhooks band (with a guitar or a fig leaf or something handy to cover the bits). It was a roaring success, although not in our house.

I wasn't allowed to watch *Number 96* either, but Elaine Murphy would come to school and tell us all what happened the next day. We'd stand around her in a group and when she'd talk about things we weren't sure about, like a girl being gang raped, we'd all nod our heads wisely. 'It's very educational,' Elaine would say.

Our school was a new one, and for the first few months when it was still being built we thirty-six first form girls had our classes in two rooms at the back of a church hall. And while our other half, (ninety-six boys) were over at the nearest boys Tech getting their heads flushed down the toilets, our toilets (only two of them, a Ladies for us, and a Gents for the teachers) became mysteriously blocked up.

As a result we had to form a humiliating crocodile and march down to the local St Pats primary school to use their facilities, while the little kids looked out the windows and pointed and jeered.

The next day, while playing French Cricket in the park across the road (Phys. Ed. class), Mrs Pivlovski perched on the roundabout and called us over for a chat.

'Now, girls. You know the toilets have blocked up?'

'Yes. Yes, Mrs Pivlovski,' some of the younger ones at the front sycophantically nodded.

'Well,' (pause) 'do you know why they blocked up?'

Everyone moved closer together, instinctively, like a pack of deer that hears, far away, a single wolf's cry on the cold wind.

'No,' said one small voice.

'Well, something had been put down the toilets that shouldn't have been.'

Silence.

'Can you guess what that might have been?'

After a while someone suggested, 'Chewy gum?' 'No, Geraldine, not chewy gum.'

'Lunch-wrap?' someone else asked in a high-pitched voice.

A truck roared past up the hill.

'No, not lunch-wrap.' said Mrs Pivlovski. 'Well I'll tell you. Someone has been putting used pads down the toilet.'

A little whirlwind of lolly papers gusted across the grass and caught in the cricket stumps. I was short and flat-chested, but I was standing towards the back, near Carol Davison and Vicki Nelson (the school spunks) and Franca who was so well developed she was bigger than my mother. The air between our bodies was hot and close. Then Leslie Finch broke the silence by saying, 'What are pads?'

A few of the girls gasped.

'Don't you know, Leslie?' said Mrs Pivlovski in a low shocked voice, turning her soft brown eyes onto a suddenly terror struck Leslie.

Then, folding her hands across her slightly protruding tummy (Mrs Pivlovski was very thin) she proceeded to explain that pads were things you used when you had your periods (deep silence), and that they should be wrapped in newspaper (no one breathed) or a brown paper bag and disposed of in the incinerator next to the toilet block.

Leslie was quiet but her friend, Sandra Threadgold leapt in quickly and said, 'Her mother doesn't use them.'

'Oh,' said Mrs Pivlovski, as if that explained it. 'Ok, girls, get back into your teams, ten minutes more then you can go home.'

The serpent had entered my garden in a new form.

The first time was Christine Lindsay's white bra clearly visible under her yellow chiffon blouse which she wore on the first day of school, claiming that her school uniform hadn't arrived yet.

And now this. I agonised for days over whether I could ask my mother what it all meant. But if Leslie Finch's mother didn't use them, perhaps mine didn't either?

I figured that the b-r-a three-letter word and the p-a-d three-letter word were connected; and that if you wore one then you were more likely to wear the other. (Unless, like Mrs Finch, you were somehow exempt.)

Eventually I plucked up the courage and asked my mother one Sunday night when no one else was home and we were eating scrambled eggs on toast in front of the tv. 'What are periods?' I blurted, immediately bursting into tears.

'Oh,' soothed my mother, 'is that all?' She put tomato sauce on her egg, calmly. 'Why, it's just a little brown spot on your pants.'

'Oh my goodness,' I was so relieved. 'Is that all?' And then I thought for a minute and said excitedly, 'I think I've had that.'

'Hmm. Yes.' My mother ignored this and went on to say that they came once a month and if sometimes I noticed that my teacher was a little bit crabby, well that was why.

We ate our eggs and watched tv together happily. I felt immensely relieved. I wanted to keep talking about it—such a momentous topic—but my mother seemed to want to watch the tv, so I just sat there swimming happily in this new Eden, apple firmly in hand.

I don't remember how I did finally elicit the full details but of course I heard stories of blood on toilet seats and down girl's legs in assembly and dripping out from their shorts when they did the splits in PE and so I soon realised that my mother's version was highly unreliable. I do remember though one day looking idly through the *Ladies Home Doctor* and reading about something called Menstruation.

'Oh no!' I thought in despair, 'Periods, bras, and now this thing called menstruation!'

Being female seemed like an endless procession of hurdles and hoops. It might have been ok if they'd just arrived outside your door one day and you just had to jump through (and suddenly be wearing pads, or a bra), but it was the deviousness and the furtiveness of the hunt that was so wearying and difficult. The not *having* of these things, when everyone else was way ahead down the track running towards the finish line.

The not knowing whether you'd *ever* get them.

So it was around this time that I entered the second (or was it third?) mirror phase.

When I was small, I used to spend hours looking in the mirror in the bathroom, perched up on the steps of the black polka dot stool, doing Palmolive hair shampoo ads.

But by the 1970s the focus had shifted. I'd got used to the idea of having hair 'down there' but I still found the whole bits and parts utterly mysterious. I'd sit with my back to my bedroom door so no one could suddenly barge in, rocked back on my bottom, with a mirror propped in front of me. Trying to fathom all the layers and folds and crevices and the variety of entrances and exits. (*The Ladies Home Doctor* hadn't been much help in this regard.) I would squeeze out a little bit of pee trying to work out where it came from, and how this related to where (according to the pamphlets) you were supposed to insert a tampon. Fascinating.

Later at uni a sexuality issue of *Honi Soit*, the student newspaper, had a flower of some sort on the front cover.

'Look, a vagina flower,' said one of my male friends knowingly.

Really? I thought. It seemed a bit rough that he knew more about it than I did. I had stared at mine for hours, but I'd never seen it as anything beautiful. I'd seen it only as mysterious parts, never a magical whole. I hadn't even recognised the flower.

Back at school, in Social Studies we learnt about the developed nations, compared to the underdeveloped ones. And at home on television Big M girls pranced around in bikinis drinking flavoured milk, spilling it down their chins; and on the covers of *Cosmo* they had a fondness for halter tops, apparently because of the way they squashed the girl's boobs together to show a good cleavage.

Cleavage: such a magical word. The split, and the join.

The thing that links, and the thing that divides.

Before: The Years in the Wilderness

It's late 1971, summer, and mother and I are in Stanhope, a little town in central Victoria. The car radio is playing 'Venus (You got it!)' by Shocking Blue, followed by a news item about the latest anti-war demonstration. I am sweating in my Amco flares and red t-shirt, but trying to look cool: suburban superior. There are a few kids my age hanging around on bikes outside the General Store, drinking little bottles of Coke and Fanta. My mother and I are on our way to visit my older brother and she's inside buying white bread, corned beef and tomatoes.

Suddenly she emerges and calls me to come inside. ('Quick!')

Somehow she has discovered a cache of 'Tweenage' bras in the dark cool of the drapery section, in among the King Gee overalls and navy blue cardigans. When I saunter in, the saleslady waves to me excitedly, holding up a tiny white pointy bra. Over on the food side of the store some of the boys from outside have come in to buy ice-cream.

'This will be perfect,' the saleslady exclaims, in the true paddock-calling voice of a country woman. 'Look how small it is!'

I take the bra and storm into the fitting room, pulling the curtains shut before they have a chance to follow.

I can hear them outside, chatting nervously. When the saleslady starts asking questions in a voice loud enough to penetrate a vault ('how's that fit, dear?') I decide I'd better open the curtains and let them in.

The 'training bra' (as it's known in the trade) has squeezed and pushed my small but nicely rounded breasts into two ice-cream cone shapes, with an inch of empty air and heavy stitching at the ends. It bears no relation at all to my body, with which I am pretty intimate, but which my mother is seeing now (in this version) for the first time.

'It doesn't fit,' I say, in a bored voice. (Bitterly disappointed.) 'Oh, a little bit of air at the end, poof, that doesn't matter!' announces the saleslady, touching me lightly but suddenly on the breasts. 'No one will notice that.' She and my mother are nodding happily at each other. 'You won't get anything smaller than that,' she says cheerfully.

I don't want something *smaller*, I want something less pointy. (And not so tight!) *This* was a little girl's bra. A toy. A pretend bra, when I felt that my lovely new delicate breasts deserved the real thing, even if they were small.

'I'm not wearing it.' Then I take it off (phew, a full breath again), and put my hateful white little-girl's singlet back on under my t-shirt and walk sullenly out of the shop back to the car. Past the girls flicking through *The Women's Weekly* and *New Idea*, past the boys on the bikes.

A few minutes later my mother emerges, her face sorrowful, carrying her parcel of sliced meat and bread. She climbs in behind the wheel and we drive off with the radio drowning out the thick sticky silence between us, a silence on this particular issue that would last for another year.

Sometimes at night I could feel my breasts against my upper arm when I lay on my side. I had to manoeuvre myself slightly to become comfortable. I loved this feeling.

And once Anthony Braccio brushed his arm against me when we were mucking around. His blue-grey jumper and the blue-grey of my jumper, and millimetres below, my newly sensitive nipples.

The no-bra look is a myth. No woman older than twenty can go without a bra and a panty-girdle is needed by fifty percent of the population.
— Michael Herstom, from Hestia

Women can slim down their hips with dieting, but that doesn't help their busts.
— Brian Ettelson, Australian Chairman of Formfit

A great relief!
— the *Cleo* team, circa 1972

It may have been a great relief to Ita Buttrose and the rest of the staff at *Cleo* to abandon their foundation wear, but at thirteen to have a bra was to control the lock. To have a bra was to have a *midriff.*

Bras were like school uniforms: what they covered up and restrained they also emphasised. (Rather like the way Catholic girls always knew so much more about sex than we did: all that stuff about not being allowed hairbrushes with handles, or patent leather shoes.)

A bra was the holy grail. Glorious key to femininity and sexiness.

Gran of course could never understand. I remember her snorting in horror at a row of bare kidneys at a Sunday School Picnic circa 1970. 'They'll be sorry in later life!'

But this was Mecca: to be sorry in later life for having worn a skimpy knitted top that revealed inches of bare kidney above your hipster jeans when you sat hunched forward on the grass with your arms hugged around your legs (to hide the stomach folds, which somehow never did seem to go away, no matter how much we dieted).

Meanwhile, I was still condemned to having to tuck my t-shirt in to hide my singlet. And having to sew extra material into the bodice of my singlet to hide my nipples. And then having to hide everything when I was changing for Sport in case someone noticed and thought I was trying to fake it.

In the end I got my period before I got a bra, which seemed a bit rough. And with it, a whole new underwear nightmare.

By then I had heard about tampons, but my mother was not as modern as Leslie Finch's mother, so when I told her I'd got my period (matter of factly, curtly, making sure she knew not to make a big deal out of it, especially after the 'little brown spot' story), she came home with a big fat pink packet of Modess surfboards, and a pair of waist-high plastic pants.

The Prison of Tatty Underwear

There is a hush in the space around Mr Elliot's door because this is where kids go to get punished. Mr Elliot is Lord of the Loudspeaker, he follows us with his voice. But his power is only that of the cane—miniscule compared to the power of the schoolyard, the tyranny of popularity (being in fashion) and disfavour (being out), the rule of menstruation to keep us in check, the prison of shabby underwear to make you walk straight and careful (not run), hands constantly brushing down the back of your short skirt. A radar awareness of lurking danger. The boy with the ruler at the next corner. The leaking pad. The sports afternoons (the changing rooms)!

I sweated with shame in the plastic pants for one period and then threw them out. I asked my sister and she offered me a belt, which was not quite so disgusting but entailed the risk of the pad twisting up and leaking. Then at school a quiet revolution occurred.

We began simply by wearing our navy blue nylon shorts under our school uniforms on Sport days, so we could change easily down at the oval. But once we got used to the extra freedom on those days (the ability to move in more directions, and faster, to do other things with our hands rather than keep checking the hem), it became a trend. Within a few months most of us were wearing the blue shorts under our dresses all the time. A successful subversion, because Mr Elliot had no rules for this.

And Then: It's Time!

In the month Gough Whitlam became Prime Minister of Australia, after twenty-three consecutive years of conservative Liberal government, my mother gave me a Fibs bra for Christmas. I opened up the parcel, expecting something usual and boring, and there it was. Stunned happiness!

So on the day the seven newly-released conscientious objectors sat down to their Christmas dinners at home rather than in prison, I stood in front of my bedroom mirror looking at my new midriff: this hallowed ground poised in between my orange-striped bra and matching orange-striped bikini pants.

I shared something with Communist China that year: recognition. And Wilfred Burchett himself couldn't have been more pleased with his new passport than I was with mine.

And so this is Christmas …

Of course the Vietnam war wasn't over, not in 1970 when John and Yoko first sang their famous song, and not in 1972 even though conscription ended and Australia pulled out its troops. Ending the war took a few more years until the fall of Saigon. (Not that I knew that, back then: I thought Vietnam was somewhere near Biafra.)

And I had a bra, but it was an interim affair: a Fibs bra. One step away from Rudi Gernreich's no-bra bra. Soft and stretchy, not much thicker than leotard material. But at least it *was a bra*.

In the 70s Fibs bras were all the rage, made in crazy new bright colours—purples, greens and reds. A miracle of modern textiles they sold in their hundreds of thousands. Sizing was easy: small, medium and large. Whatever size or shape you were, a Fibs bra would fit you.

Some credit their invention as one of the things that saved the bra industry in those difficult years. (The other saviours of the industry being older ladies, like Gran, still religiously sticking to their longline bras and panty-girdles, and cross-dressers.)

Why were they called 'Fibs' you ask?

Well, because it looked like you weren't wearing a bra (only fibbing that I'm *that* kind of girl).

Another year over,
a new one just begun …

And then, before it even really began: the Dismissal

I did find the perfect bra eventually: in a small boutique in Croydon, just opposite Woolworth's in November 1975, at the end of my HSC exams.

I had just sat my Social Studies exam, and had gone shopping to celebrate. The night before, our teacher Mr Pitt had rung each of us with advice on how to handle the sudden sacking of the Whitlam government by the Governor General, John Kerr, the day before.

'It's ok,' he said. 'It's going to be ok. Instead of referring to The Whitlam Government or The Labor Government, you say The Former Labor Government. And Malcolm Fraser is head of the Caretaker Government.'

That was all it took, just a few changes in how you talked about it. And it would all be ok.

My new bra was white, underwired, and lacy. Strong thick fabric so no nipples showed through; beautiful round cups, but without hoicking them up too high (the low-slung 70s look). The most elegant perfect shape as it edged down from the straps to the centre-join. And it fit like a glove.

At the end of the year HSC bash we stayed up all night and drank champagne and orange juice for breakfast.

Someone ran Tracy Feather's bra up the flagpole for luck, and my favourite Lois Lane jacket (filched the year before from Gran's wardrobe) got destroyed by a flour and water bomb.

Between the Fibs bra and the Perfect bra: a galaxy of changes.

And then so much, *even more*, so quickly, in the time that followed.

Within six months I was standing in a crowd of uni students on a dark wet night, chest to chest with a row of uniformed police; not a bra in sight. Waiting for Malcolm Fraser's car to arrive at some fancy reception. The crowd surging forward suddenly, with cries of 'Kerr's Cur!' as he drove past.

My breasts no longer *quite* so virginal.

My lovely perfect bra already history.

The Angel of the Forest has a Migraine

The Angel of the Forest has a migraine. She lies on a platform suspended high above the forest floor willing the pain to be gone, willing all the pain in all the world in through her veins, into the fine-spinning of her cells, the dendrite branches, the pink-grey curls, parched lips, riven heart, the soft lining of lungs

    as the lungs of the world cry out

    & the matter of the planet burns

    and the sponge of the ocean leaps in anger.

But the Angel in her torn dress, patched wings, can hold only so much to her chest, only so much grief in the cup of her soul.

Until the trees rip the sky apart, call up the river's blood.

And everything beating and being in the forest breathes and listens and weeps too.

Playing the Man, Memories of Football

To me, it's the sound of seagulls, grey skies. The meat pie sounds of high-pitched little boy voices.

A haunting sound. You turn on the television and there it is. You switch it off again and it lingers.

In the winters of my childhood it saturated everything, the furnishings, the carpet, the walls of the living room, everything was grey and white with its sounds and shapes as the ball flew around, back and forth, inside the tv set in the corner.

Replay. The wonders of modern technology.

These were early days of television and it was an art to read the screen and piece the game together bit by bit.

In the shadows of the replay I can remember rare stolen moments of physical contact with my father. My sister and I would come in from our bath and sit cross-legged on the floor between his knees, and he would towel our hair into knots—pausing to watch a difficult mark, rubbing vigorously after each goal.

My father played for Hawthorn as a young man. His six children barracked for Collingwood.

Love and loyalty. You cut your teeth on these emotions.

*

At school, we'd start each winter week with the ritual chants of 'We won, we won' and 'On the Saints' or 'Up the Maggies!' You could hear the songs coming through the fog, carried along the frosty air as kids decked out in footy scarves trooped in the gates. And then we'd salute the flag and sing the National Anthem and march inside, where Mr King would stoke up the fire and in between the arithmetic lessons he'd tell stories of how he was the one who taught Ron Barassi how to kick a football as a little lad many years ago back in Violet Town.

This side, that side …

Football was team spirit and mastery, fair play and honour. How to execute a brilliant hand-pass. Heroes and history, going up with the pack, taking a mark, joining the fray. It was men with pluck, and words like 'attack' and 'defence' and 'wing'. And magical words like 'ruck rover.'

It was everywhere in winter, like marbles and skippy and frost. The teenage girls at the bus stop with black duffle coats covered with the names of their favourite players. The smell of mud on boys' knees and squashed grass and wet leather.

Familiar alien things. Girls territory vs boys territory. Inside the fence and outside it.

Down at the local oval, for instance, the deep bass sounds of thickly padded women with umbrellas stalking the perimeter, shouting abuse and encouragement to their sons. The honking of horns from girlfriend-filled cars lining the fence when someone kicks a goal. The Little Leaguers flooding over the field at half time, hustled off again when the men come back.

There were those allowed inside the sanctum of the dressing rooms after the game, and those who waited outside. You were part of the action, or you watched.

These were the rules. An Australian tradition.

'Car'n the Demons!'

Football was my eldest brother teaching me to do a drop kick out in the paddock, practising for when he had a son of his own.

And it was accidentally breaking my next brother's best and fairest trophy, the one with the clock and the little gold-plated man with a football glued to his foot. I dropped it on the hearth and his head fell off. It was my mother's cold and sudden anger, and her unnecessary warning of how disappointed he'd be. And it was the waiting, all those Saturday afternoon hours in a grey Melbourne winter, for him to come home and find out.

You had to know the rules, you had to have the team spirit. Winners and losers. This side and that side.

My mother didn't have the team spirit. She hated football. She blamed football for destroying her marriage.

You'd think she'd have been pleased I broke the trophy.

'On the Hawks!' 'Up the Cats!'

When I grew up I fell in love with a boy who'd been barracking for Essendon since he was four years old, back around the time when the Dons first entered their long dark night. In the 70's when I lived with him he'd always write 'Essendon Football Club' on the space for religion on the census form. On Saturdays he'd take his red and black flag along to the game, and on Sundays he'd take it to the May Day march or the anti-uranium demos. He had a whole repertoire of anarcho-football sayings and chants, such as, 'Fuck off, Ump, you white cop!'

And above our mantelpiece, in among the cheap prints of Picasso and Rousseau, we had a framed photograph of the legendary John Coleman taking a mark.

Instant replay. Just add Melbourne drizzle. Once again, Saturday afternoons became dominated by that grey seagull meat pie little boy voice sound that I loathed, that made my stomach churn. This was a force that my mother spent her marriage locked in battle with, and I saw for myself that it could turn a loving man into a shouting monster in the afternoon, a stumbling fool in the evening.

I learned about mateship. I learnt to appreciate football as ballet. I knew who Cazaley was, and about Graham Moss, and I knew that Malcolm Fraser was the number one member of Carlton Football Club and that they were all fascists.

Occasionally I'd pack a thermos and some sangers and my knitting, and go along to a game, get involved with the romance. And I have to admit, when they did win, the Bombers won with style. They could play like losers for half the day and then come back all of a sudden with a handful of spectacular goals in a row. When they got a run on you felt high as a kite. It was the purest of drugs.

And on the opposite scale of pleasure: hearing my boyfriend, beer can in hand, stand up and yell out to one of the opposite side, 'You're a woman, Wallsie!'

Well, it was Wallsie who'd been insulted, after all … Not me. Wasn't it?

Winners and losers.

If you can't handle it, stay at home. And if you're gunna come along, try and be a good sport.

Carlton football ground, late afternoon some time in winter 1980. To the beat of the crunching of cans underfoot a phalanx of young men in red and black scarves chant, 'Did we beat them, yes we did!' While a little boy wrapped in blue scarves and clutching blue and white streamers looks at his father with utter bewilderment, his world crashed into thousands of tiny blue and white pieces. Minutes earlier, at the start of time on, high on his father's shoulders, up on top of the world among the victors, the little boy had looked over at us with a triumphant leer. And then Essendon had scored three goals in three minutes and a fourth and winning goal off a mark a second before the siren went.

Loss of innocence. The first blood-letting.

Well it's tough out there, son, and if you're small or weak or a girl, you get shouldered out. You get flattened. You're history.

Well, actually, girls only ever got shouldered out in social games, when they dressed up in their boyfriend's shorts and wore their hair in pigtails. The rest of the time: they got to watch. There was always plenty of room for them in the stands. And they got to go along on pie nights and sit in the kitchen.

'Go Bombers!'

In 1981 I left Melbourne and moved to Sydney.

It wasn't long afterwards that I watched my first Melbourne Cup on telly and entered my first sweep. And occasionally I've been known to turn on the tv on a Saturday afternoon and catch that meat pie Melbourne grey skies and seagull sound.

The sound of long kicks and ahh … The crowd going up for a mark with their favourite player. The sound of contest and battle.

If I watch it just a little bit, it makes my heart leap. I belong to this sound. It's in my blood, like chilblains and the smell of Nugget shoe polish melting on the edge of the stove.

And then if I watch it too long, it makes my stomach turn over and I have to turn it off quick, and leave the room, and go and read a book. Try and get as far away from it as possible. (Eight hundred kilometres!)

I tell myself I am a grown woman, I live in Sydney and I have left the man who yelled 'You're a woman, Wallsie' back in 1979, and I dry my own hair.

'Kill 'em, Bulldogs!'

I met that ex-boyfriend a few years ago and he told me how disastrous his year had been: he had failed his exams, his girlfriend had left him, and Essendon had lost the grand final.

The hardest thing to take, he said, the bitterest blow, was the Bombers. So close …

But here in Sydney people speak of football and then I find out they mean soccer. And when I say, you know, League football, they start talking about rugby. Nowdays I must learn to say 'AFL' instead of 'VFL' : which is strange because AFL is part of the present and football is part of my past.

Part of trams and tree-lined streets, gutters full of dead leaves, and my father with a block of Caramello chocolate on the arm of the chair and *World of Sport* on the telly, damning himself to hell while my mother sped us off to church in the HK Holden.

Blood and action. Playing and watching.

Broken things: trophies, hearts.

Seagulls and grey skies, and the far away sound of the crowd and deep deep inside it the close up sounds at the heart of the game, that I know exist but have never been near enough to hear first-hand: the thud of leather boot on leather ball. Those sounds that can lift my heart and sink it.

Ex-centric

I used to be the weird blonde one in the Munster family.

(Grandpa down the cellar always scared me.)

But now, I'm Granny with her rocking chair roped up high on the back of the pickup. Samantha and Tabitha dropping by for a spell. Take a load off your feet!

So we mosey on out by the cement pond, where Wednesday and Lurch dance a little dance.

Inside, Uncle Fester tests light-bulbs in his ears (safety first!). And Cousin Morticia is in the conservatory clipping rose stems, with Gomez kissing feather-light down her black-clad arms.

And Thing (darling Thing)

does his Thing-thing.

Pointing, beckoning.

Playing Cards on a Red Rattler

You always picked on my accent.

'Are *yous* two gonna go?' you'd laugh. When of course the 'two' was redundant. That's what the 's' is for. But you didn't get that, like you didn't get a lot of things.

And then the *haitch* / *aitch* thing. No, I'm not Catholic, it's not about being Catholic, that's just what you were told at your Proddy private school.

(But really, if we're talking about the letter 'h' then why leave the 'h' off? Makes no sense.)

The first time I met private school boys I was fifteen. We were standing around in a group at some inter-school Christian thing that I was into then, and one of them asked me what school I went to. 'Lilydale Tech,' I replied. Silence. One of them reached into his pocket. 'Here,' he said, and handed me a cent.

It wasn't until I went to uni and called home from a telephone box that, with a shock, I began to hear the broadness of my father's accent. (The language goal posts shifting under my feet.)

On the rare occasions my dad talked about the past he would say *in them days*, and refer to the *toffy-nosed people* on the other side of Balwyn.

(My grandfather's blacksmith shop off Burke Street. My father's clothes smelling of iron and steam and horses.)

Another time, with a similar bunch of private school friends, walking along a suburban street we saw a horse cropping grass in a paddock and stopped to say hello. One of the girls said something that prompted me to comment, 'Well, my father is a farrier.'

'Oooh!' exclaimed an older boy. 'Does he wear a big greasy apron?'

That fleeting rush of shame, just for a moment. (Well, yes. Yes, he does.)

Mostly I did manage to escape that shame and I think it was because my parents never desired that I be anything other than what they were, and what their parents were. A 'good job in a shop'—what more could a girl want? (You certainly wouldn't want to be like those toffy people! Goodness! Just the thought.)

I have a friend who came from a similar working-class outer-suburb—a few stops down the train line—but her parents always dreamed that she would go to university. It was what they worked so hard for, aspired to. One day, sitting on her bed while she got ready to go out, I noticed when she opened her wardrobe that she had dozens of pairs of fine Italian leather shoes (and never enough).

Shoes, of course. I was slow about that. For years I had no idea that at uni, conferences, job interviews, writer's festivals, I was being judged on my shoes. Like those men in Paris, years later, who followed me with invitations and suggestive comments whenever I went out walking, spotting me in my Doc Martens as an outsider, fair game.

Like the professor who was asked once how he selected the right person for the job. 'Well, it's like looking in the mirror really.'

Did you notice this about me when we met when I was seventeen—my cheap and shabby shoes? *'As long as it's clean, washed and paid for,'* my father, a child of the Depression, would say. Meaning: good enough is good enough and don't let anyone tell you otherwise.

Cheap shoes. Cheap haircut. I started to notice it eventually when I would watch older and younger women bond over their stylish shoes, notice the swish of neat hair, not a strand out of place. (You don't belong. You are an outsider.)

Is this what you spotted that singled me out as someone to take to bed, but not home to the parents?

In those early years at uni, while your parents lent you their Citroens and old Volvos and took you out to restaurants, I would catch the train back to the suburbs and my Dad would pick me up from the station in the P76 with the back seat removed for the horseshoes. Wiping down the seat with an old towel, taking me home to a prodigal daughter feast of Kentucky Fried Chicken.

In them days, at uni, I learnt words like *déclassé* and *embourgeoised.*

I learnt to spread out the times I would visit my parents so the visits became infrequent, and grudging. Over with as fast as possible.

You drove me out there once in the Citroen, your tourist eyes taking in all that had been invisible to me. I watched you backing down the drive speedily, past my father's cattle truck, the dogs barking.

What was it about you that was like my brothers and father but with a posh accent? Was it the way you drove? Relaxed, confident. Was it that faint attitude of contempt?

Later at uni, doing my Masters, I learnt words like *intersectionality*.

And still, in between all the private school-bred girlfriends, you would seek me out. And I would practise saying things to you, fucking and fighting, that I could never say to my brothers or my father. You worked out some need with me, I worked out some need with you.

I learned that in among the pride and arrogance there was a shame in you that I could never have imagined, and that no amount of expensive shoes or cars or restaurant meals or high-class jobs and travel and the right postcodes and saying 'aitch' and 'you two' could ever cleanse.

Right side of the wrong tracks. First class, second class, the trains taking us in different directions.

Tell them as long as it's clean, washed and paid for.

Paid for, there's the rub. Both of us living on stolen land. You just had a lot more of it.

I never know how to end these stories about you. Even though after all these years our story is well and truly ended.

Or so I hope. So I tell myself.
And my father died twenty years ago.

But we partake of each other. We live in each other. Just as the boy with the one cent coin lives in me, and the greasy leather apron, my friend with the dozens of shoes, the academics admiring each other's haircuts.

As we pick up the cards and lay down tracks. This one, that one. Steaming through life, me in a red rattler, you in a blue train. Hanging out the windows. Buying time. Buying up whole suburbs. A country. An ocean between us. Whole worlds.

But you see it's never about what you thought it was.

Rising and Falling

I like to practise. Lying on my back, undulating my breath so my bosom heaves and falls. Like Barbara Steele in *Black Sunday*.

I do both versions: the pornographic and the innocent heroine. (The bad undead Princess, and her wholesome virginal descendant.)

It is easier when I wear an underwire bra. Like that silk and velvet one we found in the armoire in the stone-flagged room off our chamber. A little padding in the cups, a firm grip around my ribs, that's all that was required.

Doctor, doctor, help me. I can't seem to catch my breath.

Here, let me just loosen the clip …

You said that was my face in the portrait, the one hiding the click of the latch to the secret tunnel. I should have taken it when I had the chance.

Surrendering to the breath of life.

The air a seduction, from belly to breast, breast to throat.

I felt the flames lick my feet.

Felt the spiked mask. Heard a voice swearing vengeance on the villagers.

My voice, yes. I recognise it. Rising above the shouting.

And the pain, exploding as they raised the hammer.

Don't let the moments connect up, don't let them become story.

And then nothing. Blackness.

Sleep.

Daydream Believing

The Untold Story of The Monkees in Lilydale

Davy Jones from The Monkees was undoubtably (indubitably) the loveliest creature in the universe. Those eyebrows! And it was fortunate that my bosom buddy Tina was faithfully and eternally committed to his good friend Peter Tork. Because I had high hopes of marrying Davy Jones. And it would have spoiled our friendship if I'd had to fight her to get him.

I was nine, so marrying him did involve some creative mathematics. (Lucky again! My favourite subject.)

'If I was, say, fourteen, rather than nine, and he was, well, let's say, seventeen—oh alright, eighteen—then there'd only be a mere four years difference in our age. In a couple of years there'd be no problem, we could be engaged.'

Tina and I had, between us, an almost-complete set of Monkees Bubble Gum Cards. We would dutifully stuff the musky pink gum into our mouths as we sat cross-legged on her bed, studying the colour photos, every expression, how funny and madcap they were. The fantastic velvets and paisleys of their shirts, the cut of their pants, the soft toss of their hair. Then we'd flip the cards over to see what parts of the jigsaw were missing. Each week, a slow reveal, bit by bit the picture forming in a series of intimate close ups.

'Look, this is a piece of Davy's hair! And that's the *J-o* of his signature—*his own hand* wrote that!'

The first single I ever bought was Davy singing 'Theme for a New Love'. A little-known gem, even now. A passionate monologue set to music, written by David himself. Filled with memorable phrases such as 'You're like a kitten that I hold in my arms'. Culminating in a heart-stopping, 'I love you, I love you, I *love* you!'

I played this endlessly on my brother's portable vinyl record player, lying on the floor right up next to it so I can feel the vibration of Davy's voice.

Tina and I have a pact that every birthday if our parents give us money to buy each other presents, we'll buy the latest Monkees' single. That year she gave me 'Valleri'. (With the B side: 'Randy Scouse Git'—weird!) And I gave her 'Daydream Believer'.

As to how I was going to meet Davy in order to marry him, given that he lived in California and I lived far far away in Australia, planning this pleasantly occupied many a long boring afternoon drive on the way home from church and lunch with relatives. And then one Sunday, as we were coming home down the hill into Lilydale, a kangaroo suddenly bounded out onto the road. My father swore and slammed on the brakes and swerved, and before we knew it our car was careening out of control, bashing into the metal barrier, lifting up into the air and sailing out over the edge of the escarpment, down, down into a patch of houses below.

The doors flew open from the impact when we crashed into the railings and as we tumbled through the air my parents and sister and brother and I were all flung in different directions.

The others fetched up in bushes and gardens, and were rescued by ambulance officers and taken to hospital.

But, as fate would have it, I was tossed way way out until I crashed (gracefully) through the roof of an inconspicuous-looking suburban house, landing beautiful and dishevelled on the living room floor. And wouldn't you know it! This just *happened* to be the house where The Monkees were staying, incognito, while in Australia.

Of course, it was 1968 so they couldn't risk being discovered living in Lilydale, or they would be mobbed by hordes of fans. And they had been working so hard, it was essential they get some peace and quiet. So, after much thought, they decided to take me in and look after me themselves.

My parents and siblings were lying unconscious in hospital beds so there was no one to know that I was missing. (Well, some older brothers at home on the farm, but what's one little sister more or less unaccounted for?)

Naturally, I lost my memory in the fall, so what else could I do but agree to stay and be looked after?

Later Davy said I looked so utterly enchanting, lying pale and vague and helpless on their living room floor (the sun slanting in down through the hole in the roof catching the delicious colours in my hair), and this made the decision to keep me so easy.

(*You're like a kitten when I hold you in my arms …*)

So that's how I came to live and sleep and eat with Davy, Mike, Mickey and Peter. Day after day. Getting to know them intimately. Who would have guessed that they would all fall in love with me, and that I would fall in love with David?

My favourite part was when I got to sit around while they played their guitars and practiced their songs. David with his red maracas and sexy eyebrows. Micky's smile. Mike's wistfulness. Peter's lips. Ah, yes, Peter. Of course when I recovered my memory and got well I would be sure to introduce Peter to Tina. But with memory loss, well, you know, that can take a while.

(What if Tina met Peter and decided she loved Davy more? What if Davy fell in love with Tina?)

However Peter was very funny. And so sweet. No, Tina would stay true to her first love, and Davy and I, well, he just adored me. (Like a kitten …)

So one Saturday Tina was out at Lilydale doing a Willing Shilling fundraiser with the Brownies and she just happened to knock on the door of the very house …

'Tina!'

As soon as I saw her my memory came back. We were so overjoyed that we hugged and jumped up and down and around in circles in the lounge room, almost bumping into Mick's drum set so that the cymbals made a loud crash. And then Peter came into the room at that moment and laughed. Tina turned to look at him and their eyes met.

(You know I think that's where they got the idea for 'I'm a Believer'.)

We lived in that house in Lilydale, Tina and The Monkees and I, for months and months. Writing songs and doing madcap crazy things together. They even went out in disguise and bought us a whole wardrobe of super hip clothes. Mini skirts and knee-high boots and fur-edged jackets and beads and floppy hats. We had so much fun.

But eventually, it was time for them to go back to California.

This was very sad. What should we do? After all, we were still schoolgirls. Could we just throw it all in and follow them across to America? (What would our parents say? Hmm, yes, perhaps we should call them and let them know we're still alive.)

Davy and Peter cried and cried. (They really were quite surprised to find out that we were only nine and a half.)

So we had a last meal together with all our favourite foods. Fish and chips, and lettuce and tomato and canned beetroot salad. With mayonnaise made to my Mum's recipe of condensed milk mixed with malt vinegar. (Mike, in particular, really liked this and wanted to take some home with him to the States). Followed by donuts and cream.

They gave each of us a *full set* of Monkees Bubble Gum cards (I don't think anyone in Australia ever had a full set), and a stack of their records, signing their names on the covers. And Davy gave me his watch and his favourite tambourine.

There was all kinds of sorrow as they stood at the door and we walked down the stepping stones to the front gate. (Peter was so upset that at first he just wanted to stay in bed with his pillow wrapped around his head, but Mickey talked him into coming out to say goodbye.) We had to hurry to catch the last train to Yarra Glen.

We were so sad, Tina and I, that we just sat opposite each other on the train, staring out the window, and didn't even notice when someone sneaked up and stole our suitcase with all our new clothes and presents.

So you see this is why I still only have that incomplete set of Monkees Cards. And to tell you the truth, to this day the taste of pink bubble gum makes me quite ill.

But one day Tina and I will save up our money and we'll go to California. And who knows, we might run into them again, just walking down the street, or out on the beach when they are doing some madcap thing (handstands and chasing balls).

Maybe when they are playing frisbee, Peter will throw it and David will miss it and it will sail out and knock off Tina's hat and we will turn around and see them and they see us …

Anything can happen, really.

That's what we always say.

And Tina reckons (and this is *really* wild), maybe we'll even start our own band.

Ready, Willing

I used to dream of being Carly Simon, pregnant with James Taylor's baby, singing 'No Secrets'. I used to dream of fleeing across a border with a suitcase, living in a house full of musicians. And I used to dream of you, the invisible red thread connecting soul to soul.

But I always carried in my pocket nail scissors, sewing pouch, needles, spare thread, super-glue. A do-it-yourself repair kit: predictive & waiting.

Because the glass (heart) is already broken.

The Mummy's Foot

(This Girl is Missing)

1969: *Beggars Banquet* is released on the Decca label. Boris Karloff dies. A $5000 reward is offered for nine-year-old Vicki Barton and the State Library refuses entry to a man without shoes, he writes a letter to the paper.

My brother's accident occurs somewhere just over Bordertown. The green car and the white car collide. In the white car a child breaks her leg and is motherless.

In the hospital we wait in the hall and as the walls slide I rest my cheek against the floor, which is cool and solid like so little else. I focus on a sheepskin rug, a bent straw in a cup. Later I walk out into the night air along a ramp, holding my father's hand. We take great mouthfuls till our lungs hurt. He steers his bulk like a ship and I lean in to his wake.

My brother's accident is like a small furious hurricane, lifting us up in little shocked groups and transporting us, windblown and dishevelled, over the dotted lines on the map. Unseating the wedding plans and the savings for the new car.

We find a motel, but it is too expensive. My father spends a day searching while we wait at the hospital, and after that we sleep fitfully in the unfamiliar dark of the People's Palace Hotel.

We visit the museum in the mornings, and in the afternoons we sit by the white bed. My mother says it is rude to ask questions.

I get bored with the water fountain, even the tiny cups.

A specialist, highly skilled in his work, approached the head of the corpse. In his hand he held a long, slender hooklike instrument. Deftly he pushed this up one nostril, and working in a circular movement, he broke through the ethmoid bone, up into the cavity of the brain.

In the museum I visit the Egyptian Room, while my mother knits in the park. The room is dark with lit tables. Long gold boxes with smooth serious carved faces and black-rimmed eyes. The Egyptians, says a sign, were 'great sensualists and lovers'. Under glass on the table is an unwrapped mummy's foot, withered and yellow. *Note* the painted toenails: says the sign.

The People's Palace Hotel is four storeys high. The back stairs are long and precarious. In the Ladies' Room there are two baths, both of them deep and stained, with clawed feet. We wash in the basin. All night long there is a shuffling and moaning in the hallway and in the mornings we purchase tickets for breakfast—sausages and toast. I feel like a queen as I buy opal chips in a street stall and thumb my way through brown paperbacks at ten cents each.

For fifteen days we sit by the white bed. It is necessary, this idleness, like too few seats. A penance for our guilt.

The nurses come and stand by my brother and smile. They hold his wrist in their hands, count out his pulse against little watches pinned to their breasts. He opens his mouth and they press a thermometer between his lips. They touch him deftly as they shift the sheets around his body, as if they have known him all their lives.

In the afternoon my mother takes a photograph of me dipping my hand in the fountain at King George V Square.

I am wearing my bridesmaid shoes and my second best dress. I wear my hair like a model and smile up at the camera.

Withdrawing the hooklike instrument, he chose another. This one was a narrow, spirally twisted rod that had a small spoon-like tip. Pushing this up into the cranial cavity, he began, slowly, bit by bit, to draw out the brain through the nose, discarding each piece as he went along.

One day, instead of the hospital, we take a taxi and search among the tall weeds at the Adelaide cemetery for my grandfather's grave. My mother has a photo and a number.

My parents move rigidly and carefully in this city, on the alert for danger, always careful to brush the dirt of the city off their clothes at night, to wipe the rim of the glass, to keep wide of building sites.

Adelaide is a city of death and accidents and close shaves, a cursed city. My grandfather's pneumonia; my baby sister's camp bed split by a fallen branch. We repeat these stories to each other as we drive across the border in a convoy of concerned relatives.

City of museums and hospitals, city of churches.

In the hospital, the doctors stride swiftly through the wards—their white coats, their stethoscopes. The bodies laid out for them in rows. We leave meekly at the sound of a bell.

We photograph each other in parks and beside the river and in the Square, and we wear our best dresses on weekdays, because there are not enough second-best to go around.

In the great hall of the museum there are hundreds of stuffed birds in bits of trees from their natural habitat. In another section the white bones of dinosaurs fill whole rooms right up to the roof. For twenty cents you can hear the sound of bats in a cave.

Next to the mummy's foot is a small parcel of rags which x-rays have revealed to be a cat.

We take back cartons of freshly squeezed orange juice to our room and drink it from the tiny Vegemite glasses on the dressing table that taste of dust.

The man who was to perform the next task stood outside the tent waiting to be called in. He held in his hand a fairly large, flat black stone, one edge of which was honed to razor sharpness. His job was not a pleasant one, and gruesome to watch. Hence the other workers and the priest held him in abhorrence.

The sign outside the church says it is the same as ours, but inside they drink the communion wine from the little cups one at a time as it is passed around, instead of all together at the end like we do.

Somehow this flaw in the familiarity we seek is even more upsetting than the traffic noise and the shuffling in the hallway at the People's Palace.

More upsetting even than the woman with the withered yellow skin who called to us from the steamy depths of one of the baths while we were washing in the basins. 'Pass some soap, love'—her voice dry and cracked. My mother and sister stiffen, and say nothing, but I take the soap to her and get to see the brown patch of hair between her legs and the way it ripples and moves when she reaches across to take the soap from my hand. Her toenails are painted red and there is an empty glass on the floor.

In the watery green corridor of the hospital after church, we pass quickly by a grieving family outside a closed door.

My brother tells us stories about the other patients. The handsome motorbike rider in the corner, asleep now, after being smuggled out last night to a party with the nurses. The wheelchair races up and down the hall at night. The nurses come again and touch him and take his pulse.

My mother keeps her knitting in her bag. We alternate ourselves among the too few chairs. We take turns with the water fountain.

My brother sleeps during the day, and stays awake at night.

Somewhere in the hospital is the little girl from the white car.

The priest wearing the jackal mask approached the body, which had been turned slightly on its right side, exposing the left flank. The tent throbbed with the soft, rhythmic chantings of the priests … The masked priest dipped a small rush pen into a pot of ink, then drew on the left side of the body a spindle-shaped line about five inches long.

The whiteness of the hospital, and the yellowness of the museum, this is how I spend my days. And at night, the People's Palace.

In the artificial cool of the hospital we shuffle the days like packs of cards. I spend my time between the water fountain and leaning one hand on the back of the chair to take the weight off my feet.

I pose beside a statue in the Square, tipping my head back and crooking one foot forward like they do in the papers.

In the Egyptian world, the Museum says, Osiris married his sister Isis.

The Egyptians took out the heart and weighed it on a scale before placing it back in the body.

At the hotel we watch *Homicide* on the television, sharing the common room with a group of old men, and my mother cries as George Mallaby is carried out, feet first, covered with a white sheet, from a mine accident. On the news they show another photo of Vicki Barton, and Vicki's mother pleads with the kidnapper to bring her back. Police investigate a lead in Adelaide.

We tell each other how much we hate the city, we are country people. We are just waiting until my brother is well enough to take home.

Every day, the white bed. Every day the same conversation.

We are afraid my brother will lose his heart. He lies under white sheets all day and the nurses come and wait on him. My brother's foot shrivels underneath the plaster, yellowing at the edges.

We go to church again and this time we drink the wine and replace the cups straight away.

In the museum I put 20c in a slot and hear birds calling to each other in a forest. The stuffed hawk, perpetually swooping over the stuffed mouse …

Only the heart was left in place. It was thought to be the seat of intelligence and feeling, and so must remain intact within the body.

For fifteen days we sit by the white bed, until at last the doctor nods, a nurse smiles, and we are allowed to take him home.

On the tarmac at the airport, waiting to board the plane, two of the nurses come to see us off. Someone takes a photo of my brother sitting up on a stretcher on the ground, wearing a check shirt and a black cardigan, a pillow propped behind him. In the background are the boarding steps, and beside him, a pair of knee-high brown boots, and another set in pink sling-backs; a handbag on a long strap.

We fly him back across the border, pale now and much thinner. Swathed in plaster.

My brother has become soft and white, all his bones broken and reset. He grows darker and paler: his skin bleaches to the colour of the plaster casts on his legs, his hair and eyelashes grow black and thick like the row of stitches that line his jaw.

We talk about the taste of the Adelaide water as the plane hits the runway at Essendon.

March 1969: An Australian soldier is killed in South Vietnam's Bien Hoa province. Susan Atkinson sings her way through the Manson trial. A diplomat warns on coloured immigrants. Lil Abner is appointed official custodian of the statue of Colonel Jubilation T. Cornpone.

Disaster strikes at Violet Town. And the girl seen in Adelaide is not Vicki Barton after all.

(Have you seen her?)

White Noise

Those clouds I could almost touch, and the tickety-tick of talk at ten-thousand.

'Tea? tea? tea?' the steward mows down the aisle.

Spoons clinking. Paper on screens. A new coal mine. The boats pushed back. We tuck in our elbows and knees, mind our business, hurtle on, in stillness.

Until the signs say *'Fasten seat belts'* and the earth draws us back.

'More heat!' the weather predicts.

'Nothing to worry about!' the Captain calls.

We shuffle, and fiddle.

Grab up our possessions.

Note exits.

Prepare

   for descent.

Two Stories on a Train

1   History

There was this guy coming home on the train, and he said, I should tell you some things about my life and you could write about them.

I said, Sure. (Heard that one how many times.)

My earliest memory, he said, was coming over on the boat from Germany. My Dad put me up on his shoulders and held me out over the rails as far as he could reach. He was that kind of a bastard. We were coming into port. I was so scared I started bawling. My first impression of Australia, he said.

I said, That's a good start for a story, you should write about it yourself.

He said, Come and have a drink.

First impressions. The dining car was full, so we bought cans of beer and took them back to our seats.

Next he starts telling me about his mother. She's back in Germany now. She left when he was fifteen.

It wasn't enough to leave the house, he says, she had to leave the country to get away from that bastard. But she's happy now, he says. I don't miss her. She had to do it. We were good friends you know. Real mates.

A sunny day and there's a boy and a boat. The harbour is riddled with small boats and on the dock toy people shout and wave. The waves are green horses and stampede towards the boat. His father, king of the horses, laughs and holds him up and out. A howl of salt tears like a slap … That's how I'd start the story if it was mine. But it's not.

Instead, we're on a train. Beyond the window, a regular dull movement. It's black and invisible, but you know it's there, and you know it's forward. That's what trains are all about. We get more cans of beer from the dining car, and sometime after the lights go down and the carriage is full of shuffling like boxed cattle on a windy night, the tale begins to change. It always does.

I thought she understood me, he says, but she didn't.

(Heard this one too, who hasn't? A hundred pubs, perhaps a dozen variations.)

I though she understood me. But do you know what she sent me? he says. A photograph of a teddy bear I had when I was a kid.

He says, You know I jump at the slightest noise. Someone knocks at the door and I jump. That's from huddling in the bedroom under the blankets. Waiting for the next bump, or the next scream. The next plate to smash. What am I supposed to do? Just remember the fucking teddy bear and forget all that?

I don't know what to say. It's a sad story. I was given a doll once. Under the tree on Christmas morning, with my name on it. I didn't ask for it. A blonde and blue-eyed childhood.

I think about his battered teddy bear. And how we invent the past to suit the present. Nothing sadder than the Christmas tree with the garbage bags on New Year's Day.

You invent something. Invest it with meaning. But how do you dispose of it gracefully when it's dead and shedding needles on the carpet? Why do we invent these things so carelessly in the first place?

But back to this: the boy and the train. His eyes are two pins and his skin is warm even though it's a cold night. (A rush of hackneyed images: horses, the white goddess, the bald white heroin/e.) His voice is hard and thick with love turned to hate and bitterness. The way it will be later when I'm not willing to play along, be the mother-wife he wants. Marry the hero and live happily.

I say to him, Maybe this is her way of asking forgiveness. He shrugs. He has finished his story.

The trains rolls on steadily, monotonously underneath us. You know this sound, it's familiar. I think of a line for a poem and feel skin-close to this woman in Germany, skin stretched tight over too many bones. I reach out and touch him, and that's when it happens. The track, the train, and the night, and our bodies steaming in a straight line home.

Months later when we sit over untouched cups of coffee in a Lebanese cafe, he'll tell me that when I touch him it's like someone cracking through a shell that's always there between him and the world. And then apologise for the cliche.

And then he'll accuse me of killing the only thing he ever created. But I created it. Not him. We fight for control of the plot.

It couldn't have lasted. I tell myself that, and that's what everyone says. We had little in common. Except maybe a need for warmth, a certain touching that mattered. A way of looking into each other's face and seeing something. We shared a train for a while but in the mornings we rode off in different directions.

It couldn't have lasted. It began carelessly.

Sometimes I want to send him something. A photograph. A negative of that scene in the cafe that might show the white light that burned in my head, and that I did want to reach out and touch him. I did. But something the unknown, the story I wanted to write, the thing I wanted to be—called me back and held me there with my hand twisting a burning cigarette.

But what good would that be, a line like that? A photograph of a teddy bear is all he'd see. Or of a doll. Blue dress and blonde hair.

Both of them are gone now. There is only the train, and the movement under your feet, and the night outside like a black god.

2 Another Version, Hers

I got talking to a guy next to me on the train and he said, I'll tell you the story of my life and you can write a book.

He began with his earliest memory, about being on a boat. And that got me thinking about my first memory.

I was standing on the top of a hill of dirt outside the front of our house. I had on my long dress with the blue frills, and my doll had a dress of the same material. I have this recollection of great heights. A whole truckload of dirt (funny how no one remembers it) dumped on our lawn and left there long enough for toadstools to grow in the gullies and Mount Dangerous and Mount Safety to form. I stood on Mount Dangerous and got a belting because I got my dress dirty and lost my doll.

That could be a start for a story—lots of times I've surveyed the world from Mount Dangerous, got a belting, and then found out it never existed.

Perhaps a story with a moral: if you want to be a famous explorer, you can't have a doll hanging around your neck. (It should never have come along in the first place.)

But this is tonight, on a train, and this guy is telling me things in case I ever want to use them in a book. When the lights go down he says, Come and have a drink.

We go to the dining car and order little bottles of bourbon and a split of soda. I thought it was nice how we liked the same drink. We took paper cups and went out in the corridor.

I love overnight trains, the noise they make, the confirmation of movement. Ever since I read Susan Sontag's Death Kit I've always wanted to fuck on a train, standing up in the washroom like Hester and Diddy. We drink to Hester's innocent greed. He told me his name, but I'd forgotten. The noise of the train follows us back to the dining car and we get more of those little bottles.

But I'm making this up, of course. Almost all of it. I never got my dress dirty. I never stood on Mount Dangerous. Mount Safety, Ms Sontag, is as far as I ever got, and even the view from there scared me.

I never lost my doll. Not then, later. Years and years later when I should have known better.

Perhaps this is where I could start the story. Another one, or the same one, it doesn't matter. I could call it: How I Became an Addict. Or: Blonde and Blue-eyed. Or: The Day I First Went Over …

I knew I had the time Sally asked me to go swimming. I almost said yes, and then I remembered I couldn't. I'd had an abortion the day before. So I told her this. Safe, sane, rational old me. Don't make a fuss, don't be mysterious. It's just one of those things, after all. Anyway, that's what I said, and that's how I felt, and I wasn't expecting her reaction.

She went quiet, and soft. Then she touched me on the arm and said, You poor thing! Are you all right?

The laying on of hands. The soft voice of the priest. That's when it happened. I felt a rush of wings and some white thing enter me. I recognised her at once. The Queen. I knew her well.

The drama Queen. The sufferer. The white-lipped heroine. The one born of novels and adolescence, the pen dipped in black ink. In real life I had always walked out on her agonies and curtain calls. But in my fantasies she was me, and I applauded with the rest.

She was strong and beautiful. Weak and fragile. She cried when no one was looking, but people always knew. There was always the camera recording all her moves, and all her moves were beautiful.

She never had red eyes from crying.

She was about as far away from me as you could get. Yet she was me, just the same. She was the crystal white line that ran steaming and puffing through my nights. She kept me on that edge between sanity and the other world, the world of the bright coloured lights and always the stage. But I was never mad enough to believe in her. I always kept her safely locked away in my head. Until the soft reverent voice of Sally. No one had ever spoken to me in real life, like that.

And so the struggle. I wondered did they notice?

The safe, sane rational me would reassert and take control. And then someone would speak to that other one. Call her up. Like this: Joan (sympathetic) I heard that you had an abortion? (eager) What's it like? (What's it like up there on the stage with all the coloured lights? What's it like being her?)

The safe, sane rational me would reply with the usual assurances. But Joan spoke to that other one—the one who couldn't talk about it because it was all too painful. The rare-wronged drama Queen. The suffering one. The almighty fix.

She grew more powerful. She wrote her own lines now, didn't bother with those old novels. She made up things as she went. And people began to talk.

Of course they didn't know what they were doing.

Anyway, after a while I didn't need them. I could call her up at will.

Watching people at a party I could make them whirl around me till they blurred like the faces beyond the footlights, hot and eager. Watching the sad young man in the Lebanese cafe, I could crack his shell with my fingers and watch the slow ooze of it all and feel nothing, but the faint whirr and click of the camera, the lines forming in my head for a new poem …

And yes, somewhere in between all this was the sadness. A little ghost. It would have been a nice baby. He was a lovely guy. We met one night on a train and it was just the wrong time of the month. The crunching of the wheels, the familiar noise of a train moving over tracks, and a little ghost slips up out the air vent with my moan, unnoticed. The midnight fog catches it and whisks it away.

I didn't see them again, the ghost, or the guy. The moan I've still got for any man on a train with some time to spare. But that drama Queen—she's set up house. She doesn't even wait to be spoken to. She's bad. She flutters her eyelids at those she shouldn't. She has mad eyes and a typewriter. She views the world from Mount Dangerous.

Benefits

We cut our eye teeth on each other's hearts.

That letter of yours, late at night—what was that? Best forgotten. So now I love the smooth wall of your skin.

Pushing me away, inviting me in. Well-protected, your ribs, a cage. You make sex a game, a twist. Word-play: foreplay.

Always the rules (so safe). Such a trick to find the soft centre in that fist of hard words.

My need for adventure. Your need for conquest.

(And that strangely intimate linking of hands. And those words we must never speak, written, late at night.)

Too long caught in a gauze too thick to untangle. Each wound deep and red again.

Your hand over my mouth.

Your letter, hidden, in plain sight.

A Dispatch from Cheryl in the Museum of Lost Desire

In a way we were all born in 1959, but I was a 1965 model. Of course, I haven't always lived outdoors. And I haven't always been naked either.

In fact, for most of the Sixties I had my own human.

The Swinging Sixties? Oh yes. Dancing all night with Mick and Marianne. Can't you see me in a Betsey Johnson mini with space age earrings and silver boots? Swapping make-up secrets with Twiggy.

Yeah. Sure.

I'm afraid my 'Swinging Sixties' were spent in a country town in Australia, wearing homemade tacked-together outfits and being frog-marched around on top of a pink chenille bedspread. The closest I got to Carnaby Street was when I was left on the breakfast table next to a jar of Vegemite with *The Sun* open at the 'Teen Scene' page.

And 'Cheryl', really. What sort of a name is that for a teenage fashion model, even if I am a brunette? Brown hair, that's right. Yes, the older sister's used to laugh her blonde head off about that, but who's the HTF now? 'Hard to Find'—not her.

With three per second rolling off the production line every day you can imagine how many blonde Barbies there are hanging around here.

Anyway, what can you do? You go where you're assigned.

My human was small, female, brown hair (like me.) No figure (*un*like me). Little girl pot belly. Born 1959, same as us. Style challenged. To put it mildly. (Her idea of high fashion was lace edges on white ankle socks.) High-pitched little voice.

She seemed perpetually surrounded by an uncomfortable number of larger humans. The sister, of course, and then a herd of males. Noisy, dirty creatures. One of them grabbed me around the waist once with his big paw, holding me high up near the ceiling while my human jumped up and down like a puppy trying to rescue me.

I noticed that the light shades needed a good dusting.

And that human hair isn't stitched in like ours. Or if it is, they use a very neat invisible technique.

Hair mattered so much in the Sixties. Short for girls, long for boys—didn't that upset the cart. And now so very matted. But at least I still have it.

The little humans adored playing with our hair with their tiny instruments of torture. I'll never forget the day mine came at me wielding a pair of manicure scissors! Did she think she was Vidal Sassoon? Did she think that it would just grow back, like foliage? Fortunately the mother intervened.

To be fair, my human had awful things done to her own hair. Pushed up into a 'wave' at the front every morning with a disgusting green goo and a big white bow. Or a pink bow, or a blue one, depending on the colour of the homemade outfit she was wearing.

That was the House style. Homemade, hand-me-down, hand-knitted. Sometimes all three.

My clothes were no exception; and as my little human's sewing skills didn't extend beyond a single seam, sheath dresses were very popular.

If it was a decade later some of her designs would have been considered daringly postmodern—frayed edges, visible seams. Or punk, given her creative use of safety pins.

What a time that was. My sisters and I and our humans, all part of a great movement—with Mary Quant and Prue Acton and little working-class Twiggy—the end of the Paris-dictated line.

The mini started it. I remember that day The Shrimp was on the front page of the papers all around the world, tossing her hair at the Melbourne Cup in a too-short dress.

'Like a lovely long-legged colt' said one paper. No hat, no gloves, not even stockings. Tall and proud in front of all the prim-mouthed ladies in the Members' enclosure.

'The knee,' wrote a respected journalist, 'is nothing but a moveable joint and should not be seen.' ('Moveable joint'? Speak for yourself.) And I had to laugh at the advice from Australia's 'fashion guru' Maggie Tabberer: 'Don't worry, the mini will NEVER happen!'

Ha. Of course, I looked fantastic in a mini.

(Who needs moveable joints when you have legs like mine?)

I looked fantastic in a maxi too.

Well, let's be honest, I would have looked fabulous in ankle socks and a white cardigan.

Yes, those white cardigans. Essential item for the working-class girl. How else to make a single 'best' dress do for every season? And how better to show it's Sunday, the one day you don't have to toil in the muck? White 'cardie', white socks. White shirts for the men.

And then, the white thing to beat them all—the white Bride Thing.

My human's mother was *very* into the Bride Thing. I failed to understand this, as she didn't seem to be having such a grand time of it. One day as a bride, the rest slaving for all the other humans as far as I could tell.

But the mother wasn't too bad as a seamstress. She would pull out the Singer and sew madly while the others were at school or out on the farm. White dress, petticoat, undies, lashings of lace, and a lovely soft misty veil. She scooped the field every year at the local Show.

Some *might* say the freakish size of the winner was a factor. My human's Susan (she of the 'flirty-sleep-eyes') always had a little weep when they came home. Second prize. Every year. But, really, how could anyone compete with the sister's Maree? Three feet tall.

It was ridiculous anyway, as both those dolls were modelled on five-year-old girls.

Why didn't I get a bridal outfit?

Instead I always seemed to be dressed like *mother*-of-the-bride. I wanted Oscar de La Renta, Yves St Laurent, Givenchy, Norma Tullo. But all I got were endless no-name fashion parades, and an audience of fluffy dogs and bears. With Susan, beside me on the chenille catwalk, whining about being too short.

(Too short? Too flat more like it.)

You do know we were the first dolls with breasts? (I don't count that dubious Lilli who hung out in bars and tobacconists in Germany in the 1950s.) We were the first adult-bodied female-toy designed for children.

I used to be so proud in my white nylon jersey bathing suit. I'd catch myself in the mirror. (Ah, just look at me!)

Thankfully, never had enough body-fat to menstruate. Not like Baby Janet, the one who pee-ed all the time. Seemed to think she was rather special because she got cuddled and taken to bed. But, really, you couldn't even give her a drink without her wetting herself.

I guess my human was left in no doubt about her life: fashion mannequins, bride dolls, babies. There we sat, day after day, peering down on her.

The only one I really liked was Rita, the Black girl. She arrived one day in a funky grass skirt but they whipped her out of that, and put her in a hideous gingham dress with plastic shoes as wide as boats. Saving her soul.

(My idea of hell, really.)

Rita and I used to whisper about them when they were asleep. Wicked sense of humour, that girl.

Phew-eee. Just take a whiff.

You do get used to it after a few years.

I mean, no use crying. (No tear ducts.)

But yes, it is a bit of a sight to behold.

How did it come to this? Well, a question we all ask ourselves at some point.

But if you want to know, I will tell you.

It was the end of the Sixties and the start of a shiny new decade and my human began, at long last, to develop a smidgeon of style. A lick. A promise. Grew her hair long, gave up the green goo. Got rid of the bows. Even started wearing mini skirts and hitching up her uniform. Then, mascara, a nice centre part, a bit of lip gloss when she could get away with it. Little breasties starting to pop. Just the time, you would think, when we could have started to bond.

But that's exactly when I started being left on the shelf. All of us were. Months would go by and she'd barely glance at us, let alone give us a flick with a comb. Or a change of frock, or a walk on the bed.

Boys. Yes, that's what did it. Thrown over for the oldest most-boring-new thing around.

If she'd have asked me, I could have told her about boys.

Take Ken, for instance. 'No brains, no balls' was entirely true in his case. But he thought he was so hot, and of course had to have the status-symbol girlfriend—the *blonde* Barbie.

I would like to meet whoever decided that the lack of a follicle-pigment made you superior. Blonde, brunette—we're all just pink-box dolls, average girls from the play aisles of the toy store. Same butt-markings on each of us.

But instead it's always Barbie, Barbie, Barbie.

I get tired of seeing them come through here. All innocent and startled when they find themselves hurled out into this. (I think some of them actually did believe they were going on a car ride to the beauty salon.)

I've seen them all here. Neptune Fantasy Barbie. Cool Shoppin' Barbie. Astronaut Barbie (same year as me, 1965). Fire-fighter

Barbie (if you can believe that). *Palaeontologist* Barbie (that airhead?). Evening *Splendour* Barbie. McDonald's *Employee* Barbie (right at home once she got here).

In my day it was always the blonde pink-skinned Barbies that had the exciting careers. Cowgirl Barbies, Rock Star Barbies, *Nurse* Barbies—thousands of them in their little uniforms and red capes. Then, gradually, a trickle of Paediatric-Doctor Barbies.

But never *Breast-Feeding* Barbie, which is strange when you think about it.

Or, *Stripper* Barbie. I know I spent half of my time with my clothes off, even in my prime.

Factory Worker Barbie. Sweat Shop Barbie.

How about Baby Butch Barbie? Or Queer Shoppin' Barbie?

I presume you are aware that Ken and Barbie never got married? After 'going steady' for almost forty years. (Forty. Years.) And then when they 'officially separated' Barbie went out with an Aussie surfer dude named Blaine. (Really. I think that girl needs therapy.)

—Hey, you two, get a room!

Look at those rats, it's never ending. Same with the frogs, birds, cats, foxes and lizards, and bugs. Millions of bugs.

Now that's something Mattel didn't think of as an accessory—tiny binoculars. Bird-watching Barbie. Or Bug-watching Cheryl. Yes, a bit of forethought wouldn't have gone astray.

Although, perhaps binoculars might not be the best idea. It's uncomfortable enough as it is when a seagull comes over and eyeballs you. (I know I'm a consumable good, but really.)

Now, I can tell you're wanting to ask this. Yes, I am a virgin. And proud of it. Barbie's a virgin too, I bet. After all, it's quite clear our makers didn't want to encourage Adult toy fun.

Check out their idea of manly fashion for Ken: the all-in-one jumpsuit that buttons down the back. And—so I'm told—even if you do manage to slide your hand down underneath all that fabric, all you'll find are moulded plastic undies. (At least they had the sense to put the chastity belt on the right doll.)

So, sounds like I didn't miss much, not being the chosen one. A bit of hand holding. Some prim closed-mouth kissing. The odd moment of frenzied crotch on crotch action. Although even that might have been a change from the company of babies, toddlers, little girls, bears and dogs.

Listen … That's the gates clanging.

Better get a wriggle on. (Assuming you have those bendable body parts that can wriggle). You don't want to be caught here once the sun goes down. It can be quite spooky with the mist rising from the decaying matter deep underneath.

But you are fascinated, aren't you? Of course you are.

Welcome, my friend. Take a good look around at the Museum of Lost Desire.

It's all here. Every type of material in every shape, texture, size and colour you can imagine. A vast shifting landscape of the once-loved. Or, at least, the once-wanted.

A postmodern Museum—history in bits. Constantly shuffled by the elements, rearranged by hungry little creatures. Sifted and churned by machines. Quite beautiful, in its own oily, shredded, licked and pecked-over way.

There is a rhythm here. A momentum. A perpetual rising and sinking. (Like desire, and fashion.) I've been down more times than I can count. I just hitch a ride back up on something someone never wanted to see again.

Rubber tyres, for instance. Bury them deep as you like and they'll find their way back to the surface.

Like all those items you thought you'd hidden at the bottom of the bathroom bin or shrouded in a plastic bag—slashed and laid bare in full glorious view.

Dangerous things: tissues full of snot and tears, jagged cans that can rip a bird's throat open.

There is even an original 1959 Barbie here, slowly weeping polyvinyl-chloride, a toxic hormone disrupter.

Don't you love it when humans say, *Just throw it away.*

My own sad slow slide to the land of 'Away' began in 1970, the year my human began secondary school. It continued into the infamous year of the mouse plague.

A fine time for her to forget about me.

There I was, on my back in the drawer under her bed in a nest of my tatty dresses. Completely exposed. While she lay above dreaming about lanky adolescent boys with hair down on their collars.

Don't tell me she didn't notice—the little chewing noises, the rustling, the squeaking. I heard her breathing stop at the same moment I too froze, as the mouse began to nibble its way up the length of my tweed skirt, pawing at the elastic waistband, kissing my fingertips.

She knew. There were mice in every other part of the house. Falling out of the curtains. Running in and out of the stove. (As it tangled its claws in my hair. As it exhaled its hot breath in my face.)

I could hear the bed creak as she turned to face the wall. But did she get up to check on me? I lost count of the nights I endured this.

Until finally, after it demolished my one and only pair of shoes and shat all over my grey-green shantung dress, I regret to say that mouse died on my face.

Even then, I lay in that drawer under her bed for months before she finally developed the courage to peek inside to see if I was okay. (I was naked, and I had a dead mouse on my face. What do you think?)

And then? Well, she simply closed the drawer, and came back with a garbage bag.

Feel the wind? Getting a bit nippy now. Listen to how it plays a constant delicate music with the plastic bags. At night, when the workers go home and the machines are muzzled, you can tune into it, feel it ripple right through you, get lost in the sounds.

Sometimes I find it hard to believe that I am here. That *this* is the thanks for all my years of service.

All those years modelling her horrible homemade outfits. Never frowning, or gaining an inch of fat or allowing my breasts to droop. All those times I had my arms wrenched half out of their sockets. My hair pulled by the roots. (Did I scream or cry?) Those high-heeled shoes! My poor feet stuck in a permanent arch, my toes fused together. (Did I complain?)

Well, what can you do? As my good friend, the cracked-in-the-head Buddha says, 'Shit happens.' First, you're on the shelf. Then under the bed. Next stop, the trash heap.

Anyway, you get used to it. It's really not too bad here.

Plenty of time to work on your tan. Lots of magazines.

A ridiculous number of Afghan hounds called 'Beauty' that were dumped in the Seventies. (So dopey. What was Mattel thinking?)

And just look at me! Still on my toes. Slim as a whippet. Breasts to die for. Haven't sagged a *bit* in all these years—and we Mattel girls got rid of our bras long before the Women's Libbers thought of it.

Plastic, can't beat it.

Sure, I only have one arm. Lost the other one—oh, somewhere out there. But they never seemed much use anyway.

Haven't had a bath in years, except the occasional spruce-up by a cat when I've been lying in something tasty. But no body-dings. Never had the dreaded 'green ear' condition. And I can still do a perfect high kick.

I'd say I'm good for—what do you reckon—another eighty thousand years or so?

Yes, when those Martians finally come to take over the planet, I'll be right here.

Long, long after my human's breasts have sagged around her ankles and she's all crumbled to dust. Long after the human Ken-babies have teeny appendages due to the revenge of those sticky, oozing 1959 Barbies. After the floods, the droughts and the fires, after the plagues and the famines and the lights have gone out, I'll be here.

I'll watch as the spaceships fly in. As they come to rest on the tops of enormous piles of old tyres, I'll be waving with my one good arm.

—*Hey Marty! Over here!*

As the headlights swivel, lighting up every crevice of this vast inglorious creation, I'll be here. Breasts jutting forward, pert as always.

—*Here I am, Marty. Over here!*

Ambassador Cheryl! Permanent Representative.

—*Look at me! Look at me!*

Welcome, welcome. Take a look around.

And mind your step.

Dance, with Red Wool

There's a rhythm here that I can't get. Can't get it now and couldn't then. The poem fidgets like a five-year-old beside a wood stove, feet hooked around a chair. Fist full of red wool and a pair of needles. Can't knit.

A duet: a cat presses its nose against the window, wants to come in. *Can't.*

The needles claw and drag, my fingers burn. Peck peck, like the magpie that swooped and pecked my head. (Tap tap of the keyboard.)

My sister pirouettes, a famous ballerina. The room spins in a bubble house of salt. Flakes spill from the shelves.

I have been reading and writing and spelling my name for a year now, but I can't knit. (Can't. Knit. This is the rhythm.)

Tap tap—a spoon on the edge of a pot.

Tap tap—a twig brushes the outside wall.

At the stove, my mother is blurred and the curves of her dress roll down, green like paddocks of lucerne. Steam in her hair. The sound of a tractor, worlds away. The radio plays an old song and she weaves slowly. Pick and unpick. Make it strong as old string.

She stirs a pot, lifts a knife, turns to look.

I have a small grubby heart in my hands.

An ache in the tips of my fingers.

A fist full of words.

Tracking Back

The year I turned thirteen the red rattler train on the way to and from school was the percussion of my dreams.

The zip of passing the back rows of houses. The bells ringing at the crossings, a perfect curve of sound that would pierce us in the middle as we rode right through it. The vibration under our soles.

I knew the way the clip-clop would slow to a drumbeat as we approached a new station. The rattle of the doors, the tattoo of feet, the beat of exchange and voices, the station master's whistle.

The lurch and then the clatter rush zoom thread would start again. The feathery whoosh of trees being sewn up, the flutter of open space.

I can feel the texture of my schoolbag between my ankles and the shiny coolness of the handles in my palms as I lean out into the wind, and I know you are just down there in the next carriage. And you are embracing it too, hair streaming in a long dark wave.

Everything a rush of colour. Everything vibrates.

Everything has a texture and smell and sound and a breath.

Everything rushes at me, away from me towards you, through me, over the tracks, and I want to change this but I can't.

I can't go back and show you how your smile lights me up.

I can't show you that I am aware of every movement you make as you walk past down the aisle.

But I can save it up and take it home. Every beat. And this is the rhythm that thrums my dreams and caresses my sleep and all night I hold the thought of you in my arms and the percussion of the train we ride together.

(Where are you taking me?)

I want to go somewhere life is a pulse. Where you pass down the aisle and turn and your smile is an invitation.

And I can stand in the middle of the carriage and not hold onto anything but you and no matter how much the train speeds up, or lurches, or brakes, we are perfectly still and perfectly moving and perfectly fine. We lean into each other for support.

As we cruise past the crossing lights, past all the warnings.

Waiting for Rain

Talk is cheap in this opportunity shop. 'Just a drought,' the old men say. As I touch the frosted rims of 1950s tumblers, run the spines of a row of condensed books, breathe in bridesmaid dresses and lace curtains.

Next—Lake Cooper—bone dry. A long list of birds on the board, waiting to return.

(A ghost wind shifts in the reeds.)

—Like the mice, rustling in the hessian walls of my brother's kitchen.

—And Spike, with his Christmas bone in April.

I step gingerly through a shower of rose petals that bloody the path to the shed, where all that remains is a set of false teeth on a fruit box and, lost in an untouched bank-account, a fist-full of wool money.

Outside, in the yellow grass the sun rests down on a rusting harvester.

'Just a drought.'

And the earth turns

from us / to us

as we dream.

By My Look's Caress

(cut and paste*)

I   a story from nowhere that nobody tells

At first Deirdre was rather scared of the boys at school. When she stood at the bus stop and they swaggered past like dogs, she felt an urge to hold her skirt down, a vague fear. There was something about their hands, the gestures they made which she knew to be rude. The confident way they swung their arms around. The way they kicked a football and scuffled and moved fast and sudden and shouted to each other, as if you didn't exist. The way they watched out of the corner of their eyes. *John calls for Mary at her home at the appointed time. Mary is ready for John and answers the door herself. She greets him pleasantly and leads him into the living room where her parents are waiting to meet him.* He held her gaze and she felt a strange prickle of sensation travelling down her spine. *Mary introduces John to her parents by saying something like this: 'Mother, this is John. Dad, you remember John plays centre on the team.'* One step from him and she'd be in his arms in an instant. *This little lead gives Dad and John something to talk about at once. Dad may ask a simple question on how the team is going this season. John is put at his ease and answers, while Mother and Dad relax and enjoy getting acquainted with him.* It was the dirt which they carried with them habitually; their foul mouths, dirty schoolbags and dirty hands in their pockets pulling their trousers tight around their firm bums. The way they touched each other by bumping and pushing and shoving. It was all that. It was something she couldn't name: that instinctive fear when they were all out at the bus stop and no teachers were around.

II   the characters look at one another

After a few moments, Mary picks up her coat and, smiling at John, indicates that they had probably better be on their way. Beth noticed Sol's eyes locking on to her intent gaze. *If John holds the coat out for Mary she accepts his assistance graciously. If he does not, she slips into her coat, without comment, and prepares for departure.* Then one day Deirdre feels a strange excitement when she hears Katrina Martin and George Kotanis talking. They talk confidently, like adults, although they are younger than she is. They are joking. (Deirdre thinks they're joking; maybe they aren't.) They are talking about meeting in the woodwork room at recess, where he will 'lie on top of her'. *She quickly averted her eyes only to meet his again a few moments later. She shifted her position along the room, only to find herself reflected in one of the glassed wall cabinets.* Deirdre pictures Katrina's yellow curls fanned out on the floor with the yellow wood-shavings. The smell of the oiled boards.

III   this mirror returns us everything but ourselves

This takes place partly in the toilets and partly in the schoolyard. In the toilets: some of the girls practise kissing on each other. They explore each other's mouths and face and hair in an effort to gain forbidden knowledge of desire and its sensations, with the same thoroughness with which they dutifully smoke a Marlboro cigarette at lunchtime and recess. They want to know what they will feel like to a boy—what a boy feels, what a boy tastes, as much as they want to know how it will feel to have a boy's tongue on theirs (what a boy tastes like). *She looked up at him languorously, the effect of his kisses bestowing her with a glorious state of awakening beauty, that for a moment caused Sol to gaze down at her sultry, glowing eyes, and vulnerable, so kissable mouth.* But in the schoolyard: someone finds out what it means when the boys call out 'Lezzo' to the tough girls, and the practice in the toilets stops.

IV   at every moment I am in the film

When they reach the box office, Mary steps back and looks at the display cards while John buys the tickets. Inside, if there is an usher, Mary follows him while John follows her down the aisle. If there is no usher on duty, John goes ahead and finds the seats while Mary follows. Once seated, John helps Mary slip out of her coat and get settled. Slowly his darkened eyes watched her as his fingers lazily pulled off his loosened tie and shed his jacket. Then he unfastened his shirt to his waist, and not until her gaze caught the muscled expanse of his darkened chest did she feel the panic move through her body and snake up to her throat. *They enjoy the show without annoying their neighbours with talking, giggling, or other disturbing behaviour.* She gulped several times, her mouth as dry as desert sands.

V   (for the present) I can stop here

Deirdre gets herself off to sleep at night by dreaming about Alastair White. It's the end of the year Social. Alastair leads her off up beyond the portables where it's dark. In a dark corner he presses her against a wall. Beth enjoyed the film immensely, her mind absorbed in the sentimental love story enacted on the wide screen. *As he kisses her he leans his strong young body in towards her and his hands reach up behind her neck.* She was glad she had come with him. Although he must be bored with the film, it wasn't exactly a fellow's entertainment—*The feel of her hair on his wrists excites him*—especially someone very much a man's man like Sol. *A deft movement and he unzips her dress! (Except that his lips are over hers she would cry out.)* They debated on its qualities as the car headed away from the city, and as Beth suspected, Sol did not particularly like the film. His idea of love between two people consisted of a much more cynical attitude than hers. *Her shoulders are bare, and his hands—large hands, boy's hands, dirt under the nails ...* He was much more basic in his idea of two people wanting each other and satisfying their need, and he had no opinion of a permanent, long-lasting relationship between lovers. *His hands move over her bare back, searching for the clip of her bra ...* He simply thought it couldn't exist, certainly not in his case. *Unfortunately, Deirdre doesn't have a bra. (This is a sore point.)* 'You have a rather pagan attitude, Sol,' she said after a moment. Sol slowed the car down and looked her full in the face. 'If you are asking have I had affairs, then yes, I have.'

VI   the memory of every film one has enjoyed acts as a model for the next one

Out of the theatre, John may suggest something to eat, or he may conduct Mary to the place of his choice. When he asks her what she would like to have, she thoughtfully hesitates, until she sees what price range he has in mind. Deirdre practises in front of the mirror. She wears her new best dress: pale blue crepe with puffed sleeves, shirred under the bust. *She says something like this: 'What is good here, John?' or 'What do you suggest?' If John recommends the steak sandwich with french fries, or the double gooey sundae with nuts, this gives Mary the general idea of what he is prepared to spend.* She uses a hand mirror to check: there is definitely a rise. (If only she could get a bra before the Social!) *If she is friendly and shrewd, Mary may notice that John, in his desire to do the right thing, is suggesting something extravagant. If so, she will ask for something which she knows costs a little less.* She loops her arms around herself. She is Alastair. *She sagged weakly against him as he took her mouth again and again.* She lusts after her own smooth body, her breasts like grapefruits … *His mouth claimed her lips almost feverishly.* Her hair skims her shoulders and falls delicately, delicately on her wrists. *But if John says, 'Which do you like better, coke or root-beer?' Mary graciously keeps within these bounds.* He kissed her hungrily. *She twirls around the room, weak at the knees, and sinks back, back into Alastair's arms …*

VII   it is dark in the cinema

His tongue tingled the tips of her ear-lobes. His breath was sweet on her face as he manoeuvred his mouth to meet hers. *Deirdre overhears someone telling someone else: Chrissy Barker tells Elaine Simms.* Over their food, John and Mary talk about the movie they have just seen, or friends they have in common, or anything that is of mutual interest. *What happens is that a boy puts his penis inside a girl's vagina and then sperm spurts out (which is how babies are made). This is all Deirdre needs to take her fantasies a step further.* She inhaled the maleness of his skin, mingled with a light tanginess of after-shave, and caught the drowning possessiveness of his darkening eyes. *Now she can lie on the floor of the back seat of a car with Alastair White and feel* indescribable joy *as he puts his penis in her and they hold each other*. As they leave the restaurant, John pays the check, and Mary thanks him by saying simply, 'That was good, thank you John.' *Everything about him seemed big, and powerful, and hard.* Sometimes she gets pregnant and has to leave home.

VIII   wandering like the look, like the caress

Back at Mary's house, Mary gets out her key and unlocks the door and then turns to John with a smile. There are certain songs that are sexy. 'Maggie May' is one of these. *Mary says, 'It's been a lovely evening. Thank you John.' Or something similar which lets John know that she has enjoyed the date.* Deirdre likes the song 'Maggie May', but she gets confused by the line: 'All you did was wet my bed.' *She looked up into his face, and the hunger in his gaze stopped the breath in her throat.* Her hair skims her shoulders. She fumbles with the zipper. *John replies, 'I have enjoyed it too. I'll be seeing you.'* The dress parts like a split peach. Her fingers dance across her shoulders, she twirls around the room …

IX   'long ago we used to believe in the masks'

Deirdre is at the start of her quest for sexual knowledge.

She is yet to discover that there is a different kind of sex— the hand under the skirt variety, that starts from the bottom and works its way up. *She felt herself drowning in the electric sensations.* Mary then opens the door and goes in without further hesitation. *To protest was futile. She saw her up-turned face reflected in his eyes.* Since this is the first date, neither John, nor Mary expects a good-night kiss. *Her limbs slowly weakened.* And Mary is careful not to linger at the door, which might make John wonder what she expects him to do. *His hands expertly parted the shirt from her trousers and undid her waistband, then ran lingeringly down her thigh. She watched his grey eyes darken.* Deirdre is overjoyed. Her mother buys her a bra! *She felt his thighs harden against her legs.* She practices in front of the mirror. Loops her arms around herself and struggles with her new bra-clip. Alastair leans his strong young body in towards her, he kisses her slowly, slowly until she stops struggling … *He covered her open mouth with his own, each kiss becoming longer, desire blotting out everything …*

*Sources: Christian Metz, *The Imaginary Signifier: Psychoanalysis and the Cinema* (1982); Beth Spencer, 'The Education of Deirdre Johnston' (1996); Evelyn Duvall, *Facts of Life and Love for Teenagers* (circa 1950); Catherine Grant, *Listen to the Wind* (1978).

Blade

It was when she tripped over the carpet while walking backwards carrying the chainsaw that things really started to look grim.

Uh-oh. Chainsaw? Did I say chainsaw? I meant chain letter. Letter of demand. Eviction notice.

Notice how the light glints on the teeth of the blade.

The carpet was a round black hole, and her foot slipped in.

If she wasn't wearing her diamante buckle slippers she may have been able to save herself, grabbing the edge as she fell.

But the slipper started to slip and she loved those diamonds which reminded her of her mother (who was a bit too rough to love hugely, but, well, you know, enough. You know? hmm. Maybe you do.)

And as she reached one hand down to grasp the slippers she lost her grip.

She lost her grip that day, and fell deep deep into that black soft rabbit burrow of depression.

No one knew, and it was months before they came to evict her, and found her. Or found her bones. The letter, the diamante buckled slipper, the abstracted thought, the day that began quite well and went terribly terribly wrong.

The chainsaw still whirring.

Doing the Rock

(June 1984)

the bus took off without me and I was missing you
[flashback] drinking gin on the flight from Cairns
—'trash can?' said the American across the aisle
—'rubbish bin' said the hostess and pointed to a paper bag

had the plane to ourselves our postcards and
politeness the biscuit-baked land followed us red as your thumb
[now] the American smiles sitting next to the driver caught
them up at the camel farm fists full of meat pies and Big Bill
with the cowboy hat and the bus between his legs [later] when
we reach the motel they book a room together quick work! I
smile back [now] spinifex and wild melon and the well-beaten
track and a haze to go with the six a.m. high / the big trip /
doing it / 'Get to know each other' Bill drawls into the mike so
I pretend to examine the view and make a list instead: 1) two
young men in the back seat propped up with a can each one
of them reads the tour guide the whole way and forgets to look
out the window 2) a Canadian couple with a baby—babies :
dingoes—the mind's corny as it slides to the association but
what can you do they look so straight and you wonder how old
it is why they're here (why the baby never cries) and then 3)
an English teacher with large friendly thighs who's seen more
of Australia than I have which isn't difficult and up further 4)
two old ducks Rosy and Else laughing and talking the whole
way making the most of it and 5) a lonely man (there always is)

[later] he shakes everyone's hands with tears in his eyes [now] up front Big Bill with his hand on the American's knee and his grin in the mirror says 'Get to know each other folks fun's only what you make yourself' which is true I suppose but I'm not having fun and my sneakers bought in Alice are too tight and I've no suntan cream because it's winter in Sydney

—and I think of your warm bed and cold room

—and Elaine walking up the stairs with a loaded needle 'helping you out'

so maybe Bill's right or maybe fun's only what you left behind miles and miles and I'm not even sure which direction 'out there' and 'home' make much more sense on a plane here there is only the track (always the same one) and the band of travelling tourists visiting the rock like visiting Grandma that same sense of duty and boredom and *just maybe* the thought of something unexpected but there was nothing unexpected not really we saw the rock and some climbed it (Rosy and Else took a helicopter) we took photos and watched slides and oohed and ahhed as the sun painted the rock colours that it hadn't for us and we bought postcards of those colours and played pool in the motel that the truck went through (had a plaque on the wall, I lost) and then the English teacher took photos of little black kids playing in the dust that is theirs and she *cried when she read about Maralinga*

nothing unexpected except this: *the Olgas (Kata Tjuta) were magic* and on the way back we all sang 'pack up your troubles' and 'you are my sunshine' and best (and loudest of all) 'beautiful, beautiful brown eyes' while the road followed us into town and the desert creaked towards night

'Terra Rock' photographs by Helen Kundicevic

The Littlest Hobo Travels Adventure Island

Well I followed the guiding star, but sometimes I think I might prefer my car-ar-avan in one spot, with flowers out the front and a little chimney like Clown and Lisa and Mrs Flower Potts.

Maybe tomorrow.

(Keep those paws a-moving …)

Oh, dogs, such loyal comedians. (Gauche, needy.)

Always digging up the bone that everyone wished was still buried.

And then depositing it on the living room floor with a grin.

Since You

The new puppy has eaten one of the shoes you left by the door, and rolls with it in the dust where the old dog buried his bones. The whole universe cannot contain images enough of you. And neither can the walls or the tables, but I am trying. And there is never enough room for everything I didn't say and didn't do, and all the times (all the times).

The clock steals sleep, its claws tick into my heart. And my darling your pillow, your pillow.

I wander lost these rooms and the halls of us. Tiredness like a fog. Searching for a path back. I call to the snake under the bricks and tin in the dawn, but the snake won't oblige.

And now they've velvet-handcuffed me to this life. Put me on watch. They coax me, with phone calls from the little boys. With new life in the womb of our daughter. With a puppy. Foot tethers! A twisting rope around my chest. The terrible pain of blood returning.

So I bring flowers and put them in the crystal vase on the table. In the sea of you. In the everlasting sea.

In the since and in the sea of you.

Forgetting

That year I lived in a campervan, it was deep into winter before I discovered that outside the front of my ninety-year-old mother's Assisted Care Residence was a great place to park and sleep.

In the old days this would be called a 'Home'. Nowadays they've dropped the pretence. A 'residence' or 'facility' is, after all, more accurate.

Because it's not your home, is it? That's the thing you closed the door on and gave back the key (forever)—or your sons or daughters did for you.

Best not to mention it.

(*Memories of my Grandmother* pleading at each visit—'I want to go home. Take me home.' And my mother steeling her heart, saying, 'This is your Home, Ma,' crying in the car afterwards.)

On my first night, one of the staff, heading out at the end of her shift, catches me sliding open the back of the van holding my hot-water bottle and toothbrush.

She is fascinated with the stove and the sink, the little cupboards and shelves. Delighted with the clever modifications—the wooden racks, the inverter to charge my laptop and phone, the skylight vent and fan. Loves the lush curtains, the silky cushions and bedspread, the brightly coloured mat and the gentle glow of the reading light.

I take her delight as permission.

A good quiet street and facilities not far away (in my Mum's private room). Perfect, really.

By nine p.m. all the ladies and the gents (mostly ladies, but some gents) are tucked up in bed and the fog of drug-assisted milky sleep drifts out and envelopes my van on the kerb.

I sleep like a baby. Like a child in the back of the car with a parent at the wheel.

In the morning my mother glories in the chance to play hostess—providing bathroom and toilet, getting out her china cups, filling them with hot water from the hall. We breakfast at her little table.

In the afternoon I lie on her bed and she carefully adjusts her tartan rug to cover my feet and then stretches out in her recliner and together we have a little nap.

Later we take a walk before dinner. She plants her two hands firmly on her roller-walker, and wearing her aviator sunglasses, fawn trench-coat and burgundy hat and scarf, she ploughs determinedly up the streets.

'Hey Lady,' a man concreting a driveway calls out. 'Careful you don't get booked for speeding!'

When dinner is over, we play a game of Backgammon—saving Rummy King for another day. I've heard my mother say she used to get down on the floor and play games with her children. But if she did, I don't remember.

Or perhaps that was just with the older ones, before all the spaces in her life filled up with children and work and there was no room any more for frivolous things.

I teach her Backgammon strategy, which is new to her, and her competitive streak comes out.

It's a fight to the death. I cough and hint when she is about to miss a chance and her fingers hover, wiggling slightly, her brain processing the cryptic information. Sometimes I subtly touch a piece with the tip of a finger—and she lights up, pouncing with glee. But the rest of the time I play hard. No molly-coddling.

We become increasingly dramatic and noisy. She beats me by one, and I groan and sweep the pieces up like a bad sport and we laugh.

We have a cup of tea, and I sit there quietly stunned that I had such fun with my mother.

Some days she is ok. But other times, when she gets anxious (watching the clock, for instance, so she doesn't miss a mealtime) her mind forgets to think in sequence and goes around in a loop.

I've learnt that if I resist the loop it can be enormously irritating. But if I flow with the spirit of it (see how many different ways I can answer the same question, preferably with increasing enthusiasm), then time shudders and stops and we start to float in an eternal now.

It is as if the universe (inside my mother's head) regards my replies as so fascinating that they are worth repeating again and again, until I too start to see something extraordinary in the texture of the sentences and the intricate building of that bridge between my experience and hers.

Gradually we weave a little deeper into the heart of what we are saying, until we start to perform something beyond words. A dance.

Sometimes I just tell her stories, things I know of her childhood and mine.

She listens with a look of wonder and joy as half-memories flit across and fly off. Fascinating stories. (The most fascinating story in the world.)

One day, after an hour of this, she sits holding my hand and looking out the window. Then she turns to me and says 'So tell me, where did *we* meet?'

On the day I hug my Mother goodbye, knowing I'm heading north for some time, I get a surge of feeling, a direct transfer of emotion, a special mother-love-beam that penetrates to my marrow.

I think: she is old. I may never hug my mother again. (This may be the last time.)

My sister and I have talked about how different it is for us now. That the more she detaches from her old life, the more she forgets and lives in the present—and the more the words strip away—the more we are able to feel this pure mother-love in a way that is quite new.

… Or so old, perhaps, from some pre-historic, fluid time (before symbols and words) that we've forgotten.

I think of closing the door of my house at Creswick for the last time; wandering around the garden one last time; and suddenly bursting into tears.

All the bittersweet in life. All the departures into new worlds. She poses in front of the open side door of my van and I take a photo (a good photo—the kind she likes—hair neatly combed, face full to the camera). Then we reverse and she takes one of me.

She hugs me again, for a long time.

And then she stands with her roller-walker at the gate, refusing to go in until she has seen me leave. She didn't sign out, so I hope she doesn't wander off.

There is a fierce look of determination on her face as I drive away.

And I can still feel the imprint of her heart on mine.

Always, Time

Cake crumb breath. Pressing the flesh. Do-si-do.

Your eyes meet mine in a zoom world and I am right here at home.

Boxing the past. Memories, sunlight, poems. The sounds of outside reduced to a plastic pearl tucked warm in the bed of my ear.

I'm pole-dancing in a blue jumper. Singing Dolly Parton to the pot plants.

Laying out the table of my heart, a thick sweet spread, a chequered cloth. Salute, salute! Looking at you, kid. Beautiful you. In this rapidly melting party of life.

The Death of Mr Propinquity

Propinquity: *[proping-kwiti] n nearness*

Mr Propinquity woke one morning out of a dream with the certainty that someone, somewhere was writing a story about him. This was a thought he kept in his mind while he showered and shaved, cooked and ate, like a child holds a smooth stone in its pocket, because he liked the feel of it.

Of course some might say, 'What, boring old Mr Propinquity, really?' (A bit of grit stuck to the pebble, he pokes at it with his thumb.) Certainly he couldn't deny that amid all the countless ordinary things he had done (washing dishes, going to work, tying his shoelaces), there were very few of the more *noteworthy* kind. But is that the same as story-worthy?

He had a cousin on his father's side who had once been a member of a record-breaking tug-of-war team and was able to identify his left foot on page 77 of the 1954 edition of *The Guinness Book of Records*, but sadly Mr Propinquity held no similar claim to fame. No fabulous collection of fine china, no silver-plated hand guns, no rare poisonous spiders.

But surely that was it—all the never-dones that made his life so *significantly* ordinary!

Mr Propinquity knew in his heart that he had been chosen *of all people*, from a million applicants, precisely because of this *lack* of distinction. A comforting thought.

'Indeed,' he remarked triumphantly, spearing a small piece of ham and passing it to Sophie, the fattest of his two cats, 'isn't that one of the tasks of literature, to illumine the life of the *common* man?'

Sophie (a remarkable cat) ate the ham greedily, without comment.

An ordinary man, of regular heart-beat and habits: the 8.15 tram into the city, the 5.15 out again at night. A working man (Mr Propinquity worked in an office). A family man (of sorts) visiting his mother every Sunday: the 2.25 tram and the 4.48.

'Perhaps,' he murmured happily, screwing the lid on the sauce bottle, 'someone, somewhere at this very moment (maybe even someone *quite close by*) is inserting a fresh sheet of paper into the typewriter.'

At *this* very moment? *Eleven after eight!* Later than he thinks. And unfortunately, in his rush out the door Mr Propinquity upsets the cats' bowl.

Sophie's not amused.

*

So the story begins, albeit badly. Mr Propinquity lunges out the door, his tie clumsily knotted, his briefcase unbuttoned, milk dripping off the toe of his right shoe.

Later, seated on the tram with his fellow commuters, briefcase clasped on his knees, Mr Propinquity thinks to take special care now of his life, to see that it segments carefully, that it be neat like an orange. He resolves to keep his thoughts ordered, to speak clearly. To keep an *eye* on the clock, and check each night that it is carefully wound.

He knew that all he has to do is be there and the plot will form and thicken around him, but without him (if he overslept) there might be no plot.

*

Meanwhile …

Back in the flat, Sophie has spotted the breakfast ham which Mr Propinquity, in his haste, has forgotten to return to the safety of the fridge. Sophie, who always acts on the reasonable belief that anything left on the bench after the door has closed is rightfully hers, has dragged the ham into the lounge room where she and the other cat devour it silently. Mr P., reaching the tram stop, feels a cold creeping paw down his spine, a vague presentiment, a feeling of having forgotten something. But at that moment the tram arrives and so the ham (so to speak) disappears into the void.

*

The wall clock says five to nine. Mr Propinquity writes this on his time sheet (even though his own personal watch says eight fifty-*two*). Then he folds his coat, places his briefcase beside his desk, dusts his chair, takes a seat and, after a few moments quiet meditation, starts opening files.

Throughout this time he is aware of the readers' presence over his shoulder. (This is only natural.)

What begins to bother him, however, is the way the readers' eagle eyes keep wandering away from the (incredibly boring) files and bits of paper on his desk and down onto the briefcase placed so carefully beside it.

So shiny and brown. So obviously important.

Mr Propinquity shuffles a stack of papers. Coughs pompously. Taps his pen, looks at the clock. But the more he tries to distract us, the more curious we become.

Which is awfully embarrassing, because the shiny brown briefcase contains Mr Propinquity's lunch (two egg sandwiches), a spare handkerchief (with a crooked 'P' embroidered in the corner by his mother), and a bank savings book. If he brought a newspaper (rare) he put that in there too (because it fit: not a very good reason).

Mr Propinquity blushes. He has failed to live up to expectations. He resolves at once to find some new and (more) interesting things to carry.

Which is not *easy*, as these new things must be the kind of things that such a man (as himself) can carry without suspicion, without violating the very ordinariness that makes him so special and so worthy of the story.

Interesting but unremarkable: a tall order.

1. After much thought he decides that it might be safe to subscribe to a few ordinary magazines: *The Dairyman's Digest, Metal Bottle Top Collecting For Fun and Profit, Today's Bridegroom.* These sound interesting and he can carry them about in his briefcase and read them over his egg sandwiches at lunchtime.

2. Although he cannot depend on Miss Shanahan not to comment.

*

Sharon Shanahan keeps time by a small gold wristwatch and always beats everyone else to the urn at morning tea time. It is she who pours Mr Propinquity's tea. Emboldened by this feminine act, Mr Propinquity takes the sugar bowl, helps himself and says teasingly, holding the sugar out of reach: 'None for you, of course, Miss Shanahan. Sweet enough already!'

Sharon stares at him blankly. He stares back at the luxurious thickness of her false eyelashes, the perfect porcelain finish of her make-up and a mild panic seizes him. Surely she hasn't forgotten? Today of all days!

The silence between them is stretched tight like an elastic band. It lasts a full minute (while the second hand, the least of all the hands, jogs the mile back to the starting post). And then Sharon laughs. Mr Propinquity blushes and smiles tentatively. It is only a joke: Sharon comes to life, placing her plump hand on his shoulder, giving it a little push as she always does and says (as always) 'Oh, Mr Propinquity, you'll be the death of me!' Then she snatches the sugar bowl out of his hand and shovels two spoonfuls into her mug. (Sharon, a sweet girl, believes one can *never* be sweet enough.)

This wrangling with the sugar bowl is the highlight of Mr Propinquity's morning: sharing a little joke, the sugary richness of the moment. The gentle tinkling of the spoons.

He asks Sharon about her latest conquest and Sharon tells him about the steak that was underdone at the French restaurant (dripping blood!) or the movie that was so bad they walked out after Sharon spotted the murderer. Mr Propinquity envies neither Sharon nor her collection of young men, although he enjoys these moments of ritual and communion among the sugar and the tea things.

'Another biscuit, Mr Propinquity?' Sharon's fingernails are long and pointed.

'Don't mind if I do. Must exercise the teeth!' (Alas, always the same joke.)

'Mr Propinquity!' Sharon's mouth is so wide and red when she smiles, when she tips her head back and laughs and says: 'Oh, Mr Propinquity, you'll be the death of me yet!'

*

Coming home on the tram Mr Propinquity feels ashamed for the second (and not the last) time. He looks over a tweedy shoulder at the headlines and is ashamed because he has no opinions, because his mind is as empty as his briefcase.

*

Inside the flat, something is missing (the ham!) but he can't work out what it is. He notices the overturned cats' bowl and when he turns it right way up it makes a klunk on the tiled floor which brings the cats running into the kitchen. They circle around his legs, purring loudly, their faces blank and innocent. Sophie has destroyed the evidence: all the ham that was Mr Propinquity's past and was to be Mr Propinquity's future breakfasts.

This is what he notices is gone, but because it is gone he cannot identify it.

(The story begins in earnest.)

*

Night time, Mr Propinquity dreams about the writer of his story. He is in a long dark hall. The walls are clammy and soft with a faintly luminous substance like lime. A dark-haired woman wearing a red dress with black lace flowers and a Spanish mantilla is dancing in the middle of the floor. He watches as she sways, slow and seductive, the flowers on her dress falling one by one on to the floor; each time with a gentle, almost imperceptible, *plop*. Suddenly Mr Propinquity notices that the flowers are in fact spiders, large and fat and black. They move with startling rapidity along the polished boards to where he sits with his feet tucked up on the bottom rail of his chair. He turns nervously to the person beside him: *a cardboard dummy!* Mr Propinquity looks behind and realises (too late) that the whole audience—everyone from the first row in which he sits right back to the last row he can see reflected faintly in the glow from the walls—is made of cardboard. There is only him and the dancer. And the spiders, climbing now up the leg of his chair. Mr Propinquity stares, unable to move, as one touches his shoe …

*

Mr Propinquity wakes feeling only the vividness of the memory. Which means that when he instinctively checks the ceiling for cobwebs, he is not sure what it is that he is happy not to find.

He also begins to notice, about this time, that he seems to be living his life in the present tense.

This makes him distinctly uncomfortable. Without a past, he feels uncertain of a future. Without a forward movement, he can't be sure that his life isn't in fact slipping backwards (or sideways).

The Bruise

Meanwhile, Mr Propinquity's foot slips as he is taking a shower and he falls, smashing his cheekbone against the tiled wall.

Over in a moment but it gives him a terrible fright! The white wall bearing down on his skull with such force—and in return he gave a sort of yell (Mr Propinquity grapples for a past), something like, 'Oh! No!'

Did the people in the next door flat hear?

He wonders this as he sits (having lost the battle) nursing his face in his hands. Listening for their footsteps.

He imagines what he'll say when they knock on the door, 'It's alright, Mrs Borage. No need to call an ambulance. Slipped in the bath. Ha, must be getting old. Thank you, just a little shaken.' But no one comes.

It occurs that he might fall in the bath one day or trip over the cat's bowl and break his neck or his ankle or puncture a hole in his skull and (still) no-one would come ...

Unless someone at work wondered why he hadn't turned up; enough to bother finding out. (Someone at work: Miss Shanahan?) It could be days. Weeks.

1. Mr Propinquity resolves to feed the cats outside on the balcony from now on.

2. At eight past eight, before leaving for work, he inspects his face in the mirror. Such a vicious blow, but not even a tell-tale redness. Well, not yet. He imagines: Miss Shanahan's surprise when he does, eventually, arrive at work with a black eye ('Ooooh-aahh, Mr Propinquity!') and he thinks, with pleasure, about the pleasure he will have in the meantime thinking about this (thinking about the way he will tell the story of his adventure while they share out the sugar.)

3. Note to the author: could this be the story within the story?

4. Mr Propinquity also resolves to get to know his neighbours. The bruise, when it appears, will present a perfect opportunity. Like this: he imagines being at the tram stop

saying to Mr and Mrs Borage, 'Yes, silly me, tripped and fell in the bath.' And them: 'Ah! We did think we heard something the other morning, just before eight it was.' And he: 'Well, yes, I believe I might have let out a little bit of a yell.' Smiling forgivingly. Watching them squirm because they hadn't come over to check …

*

But the bruise never did, never does appear. Not even a noticeable swelling. He begins to wonder if it had been such a bad fall after all, and to feel a trifle embarrassed about the yell.

He decides that if Mr or Mrs Borage should mention it (just before eight, the other morning 'a weird cry') he will say that he caught one of the cats eating his breakfast ham when he had his back turned and had yelled 'Oh! No!' because it was the last of a really *good* piece of ham.

*

Nothing ever does surface out of this adventure; the bruise stays buried deep inside Mr Propinquity's head, no one mentions the yell. This happens instead …

One morning as he is out taking a stroll around the garden, Mrs Borage comes running across the lawn towards him, clutching her dressing gown, calling: 'Mr Propinquity! May I have a word with you?'

(Mr Propinquity takes some comfort in observing that if indeed he is condemned to have no past, living always or for the most part in the present, then so too are his neighbours: Mrs Borage, for instance, condemned to come racing across a lawn for almost the remainder of the whole story.)

What surfaces out of this adventure (and alas, someone speaking to one in the front garden, out of the blue, is an adventure of sorts in such an *extra*-ordinary life), is that Mr Propinquity is given the key to the flat below his, and is there now with a watering can.

1. You could say Mr Propinquity is on a mission, or two missions. The first being the ordinary everyday mission to water a neighbour's plants in her absence (at the request of a second neighbour herself suddenly called away); the second being the story itself.

2. Because—look!—on a desk flanked by two pot plants, in a typewriter, *is* the story.

Let us tiptoe closer.

Mr Propinquity blushes as he reads the first paragraph:

Mr Propinquity woke one morning out of a dream.

Mr Propinquity puts the watering can down carefully. It gives his heart a tumble to see his own story, begun just a few days earlier, open there on the desk for anyone to see (Mrs Borage, for instance).

And then (*much* worse), he uncurls the top of the paper and reads for the first time the title of his story.

THE DEATH OF MR PROPINQUITY

(So if you don't mind, dear reader: a long pause.)

Mr Propinquity stops, stock still; dead in his tracks (so to speak), his hands by his side like limp fish, pale mourners. His mind reels.

He had always thought of his story as 'The Life', 'An Ordinary Life' or 'The Life and Times of Mr P.' Even, at a pinch, 'The Life and Death of Mr Propinquity' (provided it was a reasonably long story). But … not …

It seemed a little unfair really.

(Another pause.)

The plants are waiting. They rustle their leaves politely.

Having been asked to water them, Mr Propinquity does so, on tiptoe, careful now not to disturb the dust which lies thick and quiet over everything in the room.

When he leaves, locking the door and dropping the key in the mail slot as arranged, it is dusk. He returns to his own flat and makes a cup of tea. He doesn't feel like dinner. The radio is full of news, it spills out onto his shoes and he wipes them off with the dishcloth. He goes to bed early.

*

The next evening Mr Propinquity goes to see a movie recommended by Sharon Shanahan, to take his mind off things. The movie is called *Modern Times*, and Charlie Chaplin reminds him of something, or someone, in the scene where he picks up the red flag that has fallen off the back of a lorry and becomes, unwittingly, the leader of a demonstration. The audience is full of laughing couples. Mr Propinquity feels quite sad and alone: alienated, although this is not a word he knows. He is profoundly disturbed by the image of the little man innocently (trying to be helpful) waving the flag, totally unaware of the horde of angry men (communists, most likely) marching purposefully behind him. (How hard it is to give something back, how dangerous to pick it up in the first place.)

He is amazed at how much trouble one can get into just by trying to be helpful.

*

That night, another dream: he is on a tram travelling down Barkers Road when he sees a man in uniform step out of the door to the driver's compartment, pull the cord and alight. The tram continues on its way down past the factories and hotels when all of a sudden Mr Propinquity realises that the man who alighted was the driver. He tries to alert someone (the tram is picking up speed) but the conductor merely checks his ticket and moves on, chatting amiably with the passengers, none of whom seems at all concerned as the shops and houses whiz past faster and faster. In desperation he pushes his way to the front of the tram. Just as he suspected! There is no one in the driver's seat! The tram is screaming along the road heading straight for a truck parked across the intersection. It is too late to grab the wheel, even if he knew what to do. (The tram is about to crash!) What thoughts, in this, his final moment? He wished he had a pillow for his head. He wished it wasn't going to hurt.

*

Mr Propinquity woke with his bedside alarm ringing and his pillow bunched (after all) over his head. His nights disturbed him now as much as his days, and his days were wild brumbies galloping along through strange dark forests.

Like this day, for instance, when he goes to the bank to collect his new plastic card.

The bank is a grey building next to the police station. The bank clerk, a young lady about Miss Shanahan's age and with long red fingernails like Miss Shanahan, says that his wife's card is also ready if he would like to collect it.

(Pause.)

He laughs politely. Spreads his hands and tells her (what we already know) that he has no wife. She stares at him coldly from behind the security bars; does not share his little joke. She says, 'We have your wife's card here, Mr Propinquity.'

Mr Propinquity blushes. (Uh-oh.) He laughs louder ('Ha ha!') and repeats his denial. 'Dear me,' he says in his best sweet-enough voice, 'Not only do I not have a wife, but I fully have no intentions …'

Fully irritated, the bank teller insists: 'Look, *Shirley Propinquity*.' A long red nail points emphatically at the words. '*Her* card, with *your* account number.'

What can Mr Propinquity say? (People are staring.) As he denies it for the third time some of the customers in the queue behind him start to boo and someone gives a long cock-crow. The bank manager arrives to see what the fuss is about.

'A computer error?' Mr Propinquity suggests helpfully. The manager looks doubtful. The teller snorts and tosses her blonde hair first over one shoulder, then over the other. She raises her eyebrows at the queuing customers. Mr Propinquity registers the echoing twang of seven pairs of raised eyebrows and starts to feel the little pin-pricks of blood staining his shirt.

'Hmmm. Nothing like this has ever happened before,' says the Manager.

Mr Propinquity wants to reply that nothing like this has ever happened to *him* before, either; but he remembers the room with the pot plants, the dust, the neat black words on the clean white paper. To say 'Nothing like this has ever happened to me until recently' doesn't have the same ring. (Better say nothing.)

The bank manager, realising he cannot force Mr Propinquity to accept a wife, even a computer-matched one with three hundred and ten dollars in her account, eventually allows him to leave, taking his own card. 'But,' he warns 'there will have to be an investigation, we will have to look into this matter further.'

Mr Propinquity creeps out past the lengthening queue of angry customers, one of whom hisses softly as he passes.

He returns to the office, collects his briefcase and coat. He signs his name in the time book, explaining to the secretary that he does not feel well. His name looks wrong, somehow. He has misspelt it! He is aware of Miss Shanahan watching from over by the tea urn.

He goes home and makes a cup of tea and takes a Panadol and eats a small dinner. He crawls into bed and pulls the blankets up around his ears.

Before falling asleep he thinks very *very* carefully, but he is certain that he has never known anyone called Shirley.

*

He dreams that he is swimming in the ocean (dream number 3). Sharon is swimming behind him and together they arc rhythmically through the salt water. A wave buoys him up and he glances back, smiles at Sharon. She starts to smile back but then her expression changes and she sinks. Mr Propinquity sees her white hand with the familiar red nails flutter a moment above the green water and then nothing, only the sea closing over itself, wave upon salty wave. He paddles forward, glancing over his shoulder, waiting for her to surface. But there is nothing. He calls to the others on the shore (the young men from the office) and dives back down into the water, searching, but there is no trace of Sharon, not even her green swimsuit. *When they came they told him to go and sit on the shore.* He stares at their bare salty chests without envy, he is very tired. He sits quietly on the sand watching the search, which goes on for a very long time. Eventually they find the body and bring it ashore. A crowd forms, which he has to push his way through. The body is horribly decomposed, as if it had been in the water for a very very long time.

*

The weekend arrives (safely, finally) and Mr Propinquity dons his holiday gear and cleans his office shoes. He is shaken by the dream of the night but has hopes for the day. It is a good day, a fine warm blowsy day. He has fed the cats and they sit licking their sleek fat bodies in the sun.

Outside, the birds sing and he cuts a generous crust of bread and whistles softly as he carries it out to the landing, tearing it into tiny shreds. He tosses them high into the air but the wind carries them back and they land at his feet. The birds take fright and fly away.

Just as he is nudging the last piece of bread over the edge with his toe, two things: the front door slams shut and the phone starts to ring.

He jumps and looks around (no one is watching), leaps into action, rattling the door handle angrily. Sophie glides onto the inside window ledge beside the door and rubs her back—seductively, teasingly—along the glass. Mr Propinquity taps on the pane: 'Puss. Puss?' She jumps down and disappears in the direction of the ringing phone. He tries to push the door in with his shoulder (ineffectually), and then stops and listens, his ear to the wood; as if by straining he might hear the voice on the other end (who would be ringing him today?). It stops.

He hears Sophie softly mewing somewhere deep inside the locked flat. He goes downstairs in search of Mrs Borage.

*

That night, despite the sleeping tablets like two small eyes in his palm, Mr Propinquity dreams his fourth dream.

He arrives at work. The wall clock says 9.10. *He is late!* He signs his name carefully aware that the whole office is watching (he has never been late before). He moves over to his desk and takes off his coat. Across the room someone giggles. They are staring, laughing. Miss Shanahan points with one of her long red-tipped fingers to the region below his waist, and he sees, with acute distress, that he is still wearing his pyjama pants. He cannot imagine how he came to make such a dreadful mistake! She moves towards him like a waiter, carrying a large steak on a plate. Hands him the knife. He fumbles, uncertain what is required. So she takes the knife and slices off a piece. Blood oozes out, like a great ocean dripping down onto his desk, over his files, down the side of the fake wood-grain and splashing his briefcase (so shiny, so brown). He tries to save his briefcase and gets thick sticky blood all over his hands which he wipes without thinking onto his pyjama pants (too late!). Miss Shanahan stands now by the urn stirring her tea. She doubles over with laughter saying, 'Oh! Mr Propinquity, you'll be the death of me!' Suddenly he feels afraid and wants to tell her of his own imminent departure, of his story with its fatal flaw, of how he walks right now in the Valley of the Shadow. But only strange garbled sounds come out of his mouth. He wants to say … He wants them to stop laughing! He wants them to feel pity (why don't they?). He tries to wipe his briefcase with his handkerchief and notices, with great sadness, that the toe of his tartan slipper is wet with blood.

*

He is going to die, he knows this. But then so is everybody else: the young men at the office with their salty chests and robust laughs, Miss Shanahan, Mr and Mrs Borage, the bank teller and the bank manager; even the writer of his story is not immune. (Where is she, this writer who doesn't even dust her flat?) Mr Propinquity groans despairingly as he empties his electric shaver. He wants the story to continue, because he wants to go on living. And every story must have a forward movement, a momentum. So he must keep going to the office, dreaming, feeding the cats, taking each terrible step closer to the moment of denouement. The final unravelling, that most certain of all things and most unknown. But why was he wakened if only to be put to eternal sleep?

He winds his clocks (the kitchen one is a little fast). Why couldn't he have been the subject of a novel? He presumes he should ponder God at some point, but doesn't know where to begin. (He hopes, he *prays* it won't be painful.) He goes instead to visit his mother.

*

His mother lives in a Home in the next suburb. He enters a narrow room bright with knitted knee rugs and the faint glow of a television set. The old ladies stir at the presence of an outsider, a male, but when they see that it is just young Mr Propinquity (who belongs, unequivocally, to old Mrs Propinquity) they smile grimly and return to their cartoons.

Mr Propinquity sits and visits, a dutiful son swapping the week's news: what went on in the Home for what went on in the office. (He does not mention his dreams and she does not mention hers.) His mother nods and tut-tuts occasionally, but she keeps getting distracted by the rabbit and the duck on the television.

Then there is a stir as Miss Richards, his mother's room-mate, sweeps in majestically, wearing a fake leopard skin collar on her dressing gown. ('You're des-picable,' Daffy spits.) She parades down past the other ladies to stand in front of his mother, clasps her hands over her breast and bursts into song. His mother joins in on the last line.

And when the pie was o-pened
THEY ALL FLEW AWAY!

He wanted to tell his mother that he was going to die, sooner than had been expected, but he didn't know how. Miss Richards taps him on the knee and says that she must go to the Ladies Room and his mother says she will go too. He helps them out into the hallway where they disappear into a room shiny with bars and white tiling.

Waiting in the hall, he wanders aimlessly until he notices a large white porcelain vase on a wooden stand set back in a recess. He has never seen the vase before and is astonished by its beauty. It catches the light from a stained-glass window and the warm glow of the polished wood. The rest of the surface is the faint blue of skim milk, smooth as a baby's arm. He moves in closer until he too is washed in the reflected colours of the window: made part of an intricate pattern, illuminated, like a page from a medieval manuscript. And then just at the moment that he is thinking how perfect it is (how entirely satisfying the line from lip to base) the vase rocks forward and crashes into pieces at his feet.

He gasps. There is no time for anything else—people come running: the Matron, the nurse aides, the cook. Miss Richards and his mother poke their heads out from the tiled room. They stare aghast at the broken (priceless) vase on the floor, at Mr Propinquity standing alone in the hallway. A strangled noise escapes from the Matron's throat. Mr Propinquity rushes to explain that he was merely standing by (admiring it) when it toppled forward (of its own accord) and fell.

Of course no one believes him. He realises, with a sinking empty feeling, that nothing he says will ever be believed. He feels certain they know about his dream, about the wife he would not admit to at the bank, about Miss Shanahan's decomposing body. Perhaps even the paper in the typewriter in the room with the dust.

Well it's obvious, really, from how quickly they came running, so eager to witness his humiliation and see some of the story first-hand. (They had probably been talking and laughing about him in the kitchen.)

Which is so unfair! Why should he be made to feel such guilt when the vase fell (after all) by itself? When (surely) his only crime was *being there* to witness it?

*

The story is (getting impatient) winding up. At the office, Miss Shanahan notices a white spot on the fourth fingernail of Mr Propinquity's left hand as they struggle for the sugar. She says this foretells a journey and warns him to be very careful going down stairs, because a fall at the start of a journey is bad luck.

Sharon, such a modern girl! Mr Propinquity is amazed. Her incredible predictions and fears amuse him greatly, he tips back his head and laughs. Sharon wins control of the sugar, but Mr Propinquity is reassured about his position in the office (in life). A father figure: respected. The kind of mature kindly man that a young woman can talk to, with confidence, over a cup of tea and a biscuit or two.

He feels the world tip back on its balance and begins to see the events of the past week as surely just a series of accidents and misunderstandings. (A clean page: a new week.) He gives Miss Shanahan a kindly pat on the shoulder (with his left hand, the one with the spot), drains his tea, sucks in his teeth and shakes his head that such a small thing (such a tiny spot) could do what yesterday had seemed impossible.

*

But, alas, it starts to rain as he gets off the tram outside his block of flats.

*

He opens his door to his flat and several things happen at once.

1. A flash of lightening illuminates the sky behind him, followed by a loud peal of thunder.

2. The cats come and rub themselves hungrily against his legs (wailing and reproachful: he had forgotten to feed them that morning, being late, having overslept).

3. He notices an unpleasantish smell coming from further inside the flat.

In the kitchen he locates the source of the bad smell. Sophie, unable to go without a single meal, has killed and partly eaten a large blackbird. The feathers form a macabre pattern on the black and white tiles. A trail of blood leads off to the bedroom. Another flash, and Mr Propinquity sees himself reflected in the mirror at the end of the hall: a tiny man on an enormous chess board, one false move and the game will be up.

He locks the cats outside while he cleans up the mess. They wail like starving animals. Something pecks at the back of his brain: *Four and twenty blackbirds …* But he cannot remember where he has heard this recently. (Already he has forgotten the visit to his mother.) Like a damaged record Mr Propinquity lives in the present and is doomed to repeat, to repeat.

He must not forget to wind his clock! (It is already too late.)

Things begin to brew slowly in his mind (his mind is a teapot): all the unremembered things of the past week, all the things that happened or failed to happen. The Mrs Borages and the dreams and Miss Shanahan stirring her mug of tea and laughing. He remembers the broken vase and his eyes smart with anger that he should be blamed, that the story should be about his death and not his life.

He takes the milk from the fridge and pours it into his cup of tea. But the milk has gone sour. He has forgotten the thunderstorm when, indeed, the thunderstorm is not even over yet. Unable to remember even the present, Mr Propinquity is doomed, doomed, doomed.

His tea spoiled, a dead blackbird on his kitchen floor, he is angry. Not just about this but about the whole story, all of it from when he woke up, so hopeful and excited, to now, as he sits amidst the smell of blood and sour milk.

He would never go to the office in his pyjamas! How dare that become part of the story. How dare that be allowed to influence the people at the nursing home—Miss Richards, his own mother, not to mention the Matron who keeps the pieces of broken vase under her bed and cries each time she sees Mr Propinquity in the hallway.

He is angry because he knows that these things which he can't remember and didn't want are all the things that have led to this point (this spot, which says: take that breath, quick, before it's too late).

But it is already too late, for Mr Propinquity, for many things. Never to play the violin in front of a weeping crowd; never to swim the length of an Olympic pool and throw his cap in the air; never to appear in a crowd scene of an Australian movie. He will never scorch his cheeks saving anyone from a burning building, or hold a child on his lap and read *Brer Rabbit*. Never know what it is to wake beside another human being, to eat olives and cheese beside a lake, to speak a foreign language, to write a poem.

Mr Propinquity's life, as predictable as a knitting pattern, is almost finished. (Time for the unravelling.)

The milk is sour. He keeps forgetting. He keeps reaching for the cup of tea. Sophie (who has ways and means of getting in when she is locked out) sticks her sharp teeth in the delicate soft place just below the fourth fingernail of his left hand, reminding him that he must feed them or they too will die. (Sophie, dying of hunger after missing one meal!) He decides that it is time to confront the writer of his story.

*

But he forgets to take a raincoat. He goes outside and down the stairs and round the garden path to the door of flat three. It is raining hard (how could he have forgotten) and the wet drops run down the inside of his collar like field mice, his hair sticks to his neck in clumps like rats' bodies: a flash of lightening illuminates all this (we are hiding in the bushes, we can see what happens).

Mr Propinquity knocks and shouts. He peers through the window but all is dark (a flash of lightening illuminates nothing). He knocks at the window. Shouts and pleads. Then Mrs Borage comes running across the lawn (clutching her dressing gown: note, please give Mrs Borage an umbrella).

'What are you doing, Mr Propinquity?' she bellows into the rain. 'Why are you making all this noise?' Mr Propinquity is wet and cold and shivering. Mrs Borage looks like a cartoon character, a cardboard cut-out. She tells him that the young woman with the desk and the plants and the typewriter and the white page with the neat black words has gone. Packed up and left. 'She has gone to Perth,' Mrs Borage shouts. (Do you hear? No one there!)

He takes this in slowly. One small black word at a time. He chews his moustache. It has taken him all these years (all these pages) to get angry at something (to grow a moustache), to question just one thing: a small thing like the title of a story because it is his. And now he is being told that the story and the writer have gone, that the room where it all began is empty. (His life a driverless tram.) *That he is making all this noise and disturbing everyone over nothing.*

'Go inside, Mr Propinquity,' Mrs Borage says. 'You'll catch your death out here.'

He feels tears welling in his eyes, tastes the salt in his teeth. He wants to say that he has already caught his death—a few weeks ago in that room. But Mrs Borage is talking about the rain which soaks through his clothes, putting its cold clammy fingers around his neck. She would say that 'catching your death' is just a figure of speech. Words: like 'being the death of someone' or 'being embarrassed to death' or 'laughing your head off.'

He returns slowly and painfully to his flat. If the story began in the room below with the plants and the dust, it also began here. He goes inside with his wet clothes and his teeth chattering. There is no milk for a cup of tea. No violins, just Sophie wailing. His chest aches. His bones, his head. Sophie and the other cat (who may as well remain nameless now) share the best seat by the heater, while Mr Propinquity sits on the one with the broken springs.

He sits with his elbows on his knees and his hands clenched under his chin (so much thinner these days, he had hardly noticed), and listens to the rain and the soft splutter of the gas. He imagines a car on a highway over to Perth—a place he knows exists but has never seen—and in the boot of the car, a suitcase, a ream of white paper, a typewriter.

What are Mr Propinquity's last thoughts having caught his death in the rain?

He notices the spot on the nail of his fourth finger and wonders whose journey it foretells.

Sophie is wailing. He has read stories of old people who die in their homes and are eaten by their pets. He can tell from the malicious gleam in Sophie's eye that she has never loved him.

He wishes he had a pillow for his head.

He wished it wasn't going to hurt.

When You Hold Me

(The Bra Monologues)

With a bra, I don't need you. I feel feminine. I can keep remembering (watching television, doing the dishes, leaning over to pick up the paper) that I have breasts. That these are desirable objects. That *I* am desirable.

I feel contained, defined. Firm, solid. A woman, not a girl.

And when I take it off at night I feel all the fleshiness and softness of my inside form, my private body.

*

I like wearing a bra around the house. I am wearing one now as I type. It is like a tight band holding me around my chest, just under my breasts: the underwire circles and defines them, points them out to the world, to you, myself, reminds me of who I am.

*

My favourite bra is black with under-wiring, like two half-moons that shape and lift, and it has a black eyehole-cotton-lace bodice, with old-fashioned vertical boning going all the way down to my waist, keeping it in place, keeping me upright, graceful, reminding me of my bondage, my servitude, my exquisite place in the world, my fragility, the delicate whiteness of my bones and flesh underneath all this wire and lace and fabric, my suppleness, my flesh, my skin, the blood that is faintly constricted, my breath that comes more as a slight pant, my incredible strength and resilience that I can wear such a thing and survive, that I can still be free inside of it, that inside I am private, myself, a secret self that you don't know about, and that you might want.

I am protected, behind bars. I am safe. I am…

*

I am an exotic hothouse flower, take off these clothes and I will fall down, bruise easily. I am tough, because I can wear these garments which would make you faint.

*

I feel suffocated, I want to scream. I feel like someone is pulling at me, reined in when I want to move and run, I want to tear at the bit and struggle against these straps and tiny finger-defying hooks. I am furious, white foam at my lips. I want to run till my heart bursts …

*

When I take off my bra at night, my flesh sags out, my form dissolves, my breath expels, my shape disintegrates. I deflate, become a formless mass. A fleshy blob of tissue and skin and fat fat fat. I am shapeless. I am everywhere. My breasts shrink, they float back against my ribs, dissolving like a moon in water. I am so indefinite now. I am no longer Jane Russell (in miniature), I am just me. Nobody.

*

I look at myself in the mirror when I wear my bra and suddenly I no longer like the thickness of my waist. I am part way there to being the shape that is fashionable, but the rest of me is out of place. The wrong shape. The new breasts don't match the old waist and hips. (I need a girdle. I need a New Body.)

*

I look more professional in my new silk shirt when I wear a bra, not soft and nipple-showing and formless, but hard-lined and definite, a woman who can safely take on the men, mix with the boys. Protected, armour-plated, secure, phallic with the best of them.

My new bra is called a bombshell, and it has a miniature metal bomb sewn onto the valley between my breasts. My sports bra is called Sports Jock.

(My Joan of Arc.)

My bra gives me balls.

My shoulder pads give me muscles.

My high heels give me stature.

My red mouth is moist and ready, signals that I am what I make myself, my brave face, my lucky amulet, my mouth which can hiss, sneer, pout, smile, laugh, kiss, bite, sting, and speak.

My bra makes me feel feminine, powerful.

My red lips make me feel sexy.

(You make me so weak.)

Hold me tight. I need you.

*

When I take off my bra at night, for a long time afterwards it feels as if I have someone's arms wrapped around me, cupping my breasts in strong palms, thick hard fingers holding me in place, imprinting on my flesh, making me real.

*

I keep thinking of your fingers unclipping my suspenders, running your hands along the inside of my thigh where it is soft and white.

I want to gasp, but I can hardly breathe.

I put my knee between your legs as we dance. I know what you're thinking.

*

I feel breathless.

I feel afraid. Choking. Delicate and weak. Strong like iron, like steel wires, impenetrable.

To get access to me you have to take off something first. You have to do some work, learn to manoeuvre the delicate tricky hooks and eyes that are so foreign to your sex, you have to learn some of my secrets. You have to be patient.

You are so clumsy.

Here, let me do it.

*

I unwrap myself from your embrace, my breasts fall forward to try to touch you as you move away, my muscles expand and shudder, the skin tingles where your bones bit into my flesh, the blood begins to circulate all over again like new life, my body joins up with itself, I take a deep breath. I put on something slinky. I slide in between the sheets.

I fall asleep with your silhouette watching over my bedside chair. The shape of me, vigilant. My vigilante.

*

And I will wear a black wonder-bra, and black suspenders, and lavender nickers and purple lipstick. And I will cut off one of my breasts to fire the arrow. And I will carry a big stick.

*

And I keep your love letters in my favourite bra, tucked close to my heart, the pulse at the lip, the white crease—the red bra with the satin stitching and the bow in the middle. It is almost midnight! The party is about to begin. I can hear the fireworks over the river. (Shh shh, let me think …)

And I will wait for you.

I will wait for you by the shore.

On Turning Sixty and After Shingles

'If your builder could place a small red bird
in your chest to beat as your heart …'
— Natalie Diaz, from 'The First Water is the Body'

If the builder placed a bird in my chest it would be like the bewildered and terrified head of the tiny duckling rising above the swirling creek, then plunged down into the current; then rising up to see the world still here, still turning; then down again.

How many more of these breaths do I have left to me before the jaws of the eel find my soft feet and take me down one last time?

When the eel lifts us up to the surface, trying to dislodge us, to find purchase, we have one small moment to look about—at the sky, the grass, the surface of the water blackening in the dusk, the rocks along the edge, the reeds where it all began.

Take that moment and use it. Embrace it.

If you fear its loss, you'll miss it.

Then when the eel plunges you under and your beak fills with iced water, surrender to it. Hold on. Be ready. Because eventually it will lift you up again, trying to find you as you cling to its back.

Be ready to embrace the sky.

Be ready to stare the stranger on the bank in the eye.

She cannot help you but, for this moment, you are one.

In the Hologram Forest

(2042)

She says, If we make a space for them, create a moment of habitat, will they return do you think? A water bowl, a tree they like with fruit, soil for worms and grubs. Prickle bushes for safety.

He says, The trick is to hold them in your thoughts. Merge the components as a thought-animal. See how it takes up residence, see how it alters things. The top tier predators, so essential. The small and the swift-footed. The moss and lichen.

Create an ecology with your mind.

*

But in the hologram forest, the air is humid with loss.

At night when she leaves the room where the others watch ancient videos of *The Beverly Hillbillies* and *Mr Ed* (a horse is a horse) she seeks him out in the tech wing.

They lie under the dome and watch real stars. (Real stars. Dead stars.)

Are they real? Or is this part of the hologram? She doesn't ask.

The forest sounds have been getting louder, menacing sometimes.

He is angry with her. She cannot give him what he wants. She is good at spotting who will survive and who won't.

*

What does it mean to love a particular being—a tree, or a certain animal or bird—when it no longer exists? (When the thread of that love is sliced clean through?)

*

In her sealed sleeping capsule she writes in her diary: Lately when I go into the hologram forest it is as if the creatures are aware of me. The kookaburra alights on a branch and stares. The water dragons shuffle closer, raising a front leg (ta ta), the warning-off wave (You—time to go!). The dingoes sniff the air, they turn their heads in my direction. The kangaroos bound away.

Are they able to think, these echoes and figments of the past?

What do they see when they look at me?

*

Fear becomes a claw.

(What have we done? Am I doing this?)

*

He says, Are you frightened for them?

(What is it makes them sniff the air, do they know what is coming?)

Or are you frightened for yourself—for us—for what we have become?

*

She says, Is the forest about them, or is it about me?

He says, Is it even a forest if it exists only for us; if there is no them?

The True Story of
an Escape Artist

'You should count yourself lucky, dear. some girls have families who are so terrible they end up seeing psychiatrists.*'*

Jackie: *'Twice a week, Mum!'*

Later, to Roseanne: *'She had me backed into a corner. I* had *to hurt her.'*

BLOODLINES

The first photo is 'everybody' at Grandma Beattie's seventieth birthday in 1959. The nineteen grandchildren. I'm one of the three babies held by the older boys in the back row.

Five of these people are my siblings.

You can tell which ones we are because we all have the same deep dimple in our chins and the same little gutter running from nose to lips. ('This one's a Spencer,' says the nurse, pressing her finger firmly in the soft putty of our faces to make the trademark before the doctor cuts the umbilical cord.)

So even Robbie, my eldest brother, and I—distant specks at either end of the table for six years until he married and moved away—would recognise each other if we met on the street. Or at a wedding. Or Christmas (if he can get away from the milking in time).

Aren't we good children. Imagine trying to do this now—get nineteen children, babies and teenagers sitting quietly together, smiling, and still enough to have a photo taken.

Of course, conscription began a few years later and Australia got involved in the Vietnam war, as my Grandmother could have predicted as soon as the first ten of her grandchildren were boys: God's way of preparing for a war in twenty years time.

Between them, the people in this photo have produced a further forty children and several grandchildren. Only two of the nineteen have remained childless; one has never married.

(Guess which one is me.)

*

But I'm only in this family by accident (anyway). It was all a mistake really …

*

I have a fantasy life under the house.

I swing on the little gate that leads under the brick verandah and pretend it is my horse (faster than the wind). I have a piece of hay-band tied surreptitiously to the top rung for the reins, and when my mother appears suddenly at the back door I am ready to leap off. I feign nonchalance ('just looking for something') and she believes me. I crawl back up under the house, far up under the kitchen and the bathroom where the earth is polished and dry like the bones sucked clean by the dogs who come up to the house at the end of the day dripping dam water, shaking their tails and waiting to be fed.

I am ashamed because I am frightened of the cows as I walk through the house paddock. And sometimes I can't jump the little fence at the bottom of the lawn as we run for the school bus. I can do it sometimes, but sometimes I think too much and then forget. I don't know how to move my legs, I don't know which foot to lift first and I have to stop and straddle the fence, and then I am late and they have to wait for me.

*

Permutations and combinations: in a family of eight (two parents, six children) you have literally hundreds of relations. For instance there are 28 different couple combinations; plus 56 three-way combinations, with each person involved in a possible 21 triangles.

The family is a reproducer of bodies: big ones, small, 'male', 'female', young and old; all rubbing up against each other, year after year. So many clutches, touches, holds. Each body gets marked out into zones. Imprinted with all the hands that pass it around as a baby. Absorbing the family ills like carb soda placed in the fridge. Shhh. Don't talk about it. Nothing's wrong.

FAMILY SECRETS / ESCAPE ROUTES

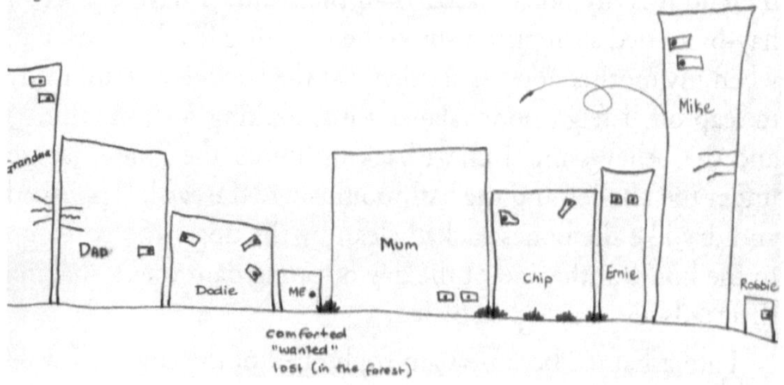

This is a portrait of my family (drawn for my therapist).

I'm nine. I'm the little one with the door handle, in among the forest of tall buildings. See the cracks, and the grass growing up between some of them. (See the eyes.)

'Which way does the door open?' asked Phil.

'Inwards.'

*

The baby is adored; the baby is hated for getting all that attention when there is so little around. (So spoilt!)

If only the baby would go away, or had never been born; the baby is wanted desperately (come here baby, give me a cuddle).

*

The door says: 'Let me go.'

But it says it so softly, no one hears.

*

The thing about being the last in a big family is that there is so *much* of it already there, already in motion before you even set foot in it.

It swirls around my ankles, a thick current, knocking me off my feet.

*

Another secret door

Inside the daggiest house in the world was a long grey-linoed hallway, shiny with floor wax, where we played blind-man's bluff and hide-and-seek and dress ups. There were ten doors coming off this hallway and a bend at either end. Doors for the bedrooms, the bathroom, the two wardrobes (one for the boys and one for the girls), the rarely used front door with its bevelled glass panel, the linen closet where a bat flew out, and the two doors to the living area where we would hide and watch *Homicide* through the cracks after we'd been sent to bed (a family tradition).

In the little space between the two wardrobe doors was the entrance to my secret stairway down to two stone rooms full of sumptuous velvet dresses and gilt mirrors and people who were always glad to see me when I went there at night.

It smelt of toast and damp socks. Dream smells.

*

My mother works so hard; till eleven at night in the kitchen, until my father's snores finally drift up the hallway. And then she is awake and up before him at dawn, stirring the porridge. In the evenings she sits on the couch and knits.

If you try to get close, needles and elbows stick into your arms. Or sometimes she lets me in beside her, for a treat. She is so tired she sleeps in the afternoons when everyone else is away at school. I stand guard by the window, peering through the venetians, ready to wake her when the school bus appears at the bend.

Six babies: one, two, three, four, five—a girl!, six—another girl. (A change is coming, but *when?*)

It has to end somewhere.

It ended with me.

*

Everyone sits on the one younger than them.

(Wahh!)

Every new child climbs onto the shoulders of the one before it.

The youngest gets to climb up higher than all the others, and gets a view way over the paddocks, way over the dairy, down the road and off around the bend.

Big brother's long legs squelching in black gum boots, swaying like an elephant, she grips her fingers in his hair. She is the straw that broke the camel's back.

168

She is profoundly unsafe; absurdly powerful.

*

Every family needs a baby. 'Grow up!' everyone tells the baby, but as long as there is a baby the parents can still be parents, the family can still function. The baby knows this, it's coded into her body.

The baby must never be allowed to grow up. Mummy and Daddy must never be allowed to leave home.

*

At the end of the line a lot of debris and rubbish collects, but what do you do with it? There's no one to pass it on to, it's yours. It sticks to your body, becomes so familiar that you think you must have been born with it.

… Well, of course you were born with it, in a sense.

*

In my fantasy stable under the house, I had a superlative horse named Ajax (after the cleaning powder).

A coal black stallion (of course—all superlative horses are stallions, aren't they? I thought that's what the word meant). Taking hold of my hay-band reins and using the slats as stirrups, I climb up and away we go. (Sometimes, if there is a fire, or a robbery, I have to run and leap up on him and he is moving before my bottom hits the saddle.) I never fall off—even when we have to jump six foot fences, although I kind of tip forward in my seat and have to balance myself back up again. ('Good on you, Ajax, now, run like the wind!')

My mother appears suddenly at the back door with a basket of washing on her hip. I stand with my hand resting lightly on the little gate. ('Just going under the house to get something …')

I crawl back up under the house, I like the spot right up under the kitchen where it is too low for anyone else.

('Time to go to sleep now, Ajax. That's it, good boy, be calm now. That's it, Ajax.' Sometimes he would be restless and knock in his stable at night. I would get up and take him food, some oats. Sometimes he just needed a pat, or to hear my voice close and warm and breathy in his ear.)

*

Every family needs an unreproductive one: a spinster aunt.

I phone my brothers and sister and they answer with, 'Hello, Little Sister.' My father: 'Hello Baby Daughter.'

They say: 'Are you working?' I say no, just writing. Or studying. (Un-productive, too.)

They make jokes about the colour of my hair and what it will be next time they see me. (The blonde, black and red sheep.)

One of my nephews was sixteen before he realised I was actually his father's sister and not some strange distant relation turning up each Christmas.

*

What's wrong?

Nothing's wrong.

*

There are so many people. The baby tries very hard not to need anything herself.

*

Family Secrets 2

There are ghosts in the ceiling: listen!

(From far away …)

> *She'll be coming round the mountain when she comes …*
> *She'll be riding six white horses,*
> *She'll be wearing pink pyjamas,*
> *and we'll all go to meet her when she comes.*

She was Effie, my father's mother. Racketing round the mountain bends, six foaming horses straining at the leads, white as clouds, chenille dressing grown flapping in the wind. Coming down from heaven to join us at the family dinner table. But she never arrived.

What if she had?

('Come and look at my horse Ajax, Grandma.')

This song used to excite me in the same way Santa Claus did, listening for his sleigh on the gravel driveway …

And then about eight years ago I was shown a photo of three very stern, dark, Scottish sisters standing shoulder to shoulder against a brick wall in winter coats and hats, and was told that one of them was my grandmother.

The Effie with the pink pyjamas and white cloudy hair streaming in the wind veered off round the corner and disappeared and the second Effie came into view, squat and broad. A kill-joy if her photo was anything to go on which my mother says it wasn't. 'She was a *lovely* woman,' my mother says, as if to suggest she didn't deserve the family she got. My father's side: the city side, containing butchers and factory workers as well as Uncle Bill the ladies man, and a couple of divorcees.

('What did Uncle Bill do, Dad?'

'Nothing he couldn't get out of.')

We used to visit them in the early days but gradually lost contact. After her death in 1951, and her husband's a few years later, there were various fallings out; the eight children fragmented, cracked, scattered about.

So there is this family too, the Other side, the rough angry wild side. With Neil, for instance, with his 'Temporary Australian' sign pinned above his bedroom door, killing himself on a borrowed motorbike on his sixteenth birthday.

The hidden censored family, gradually erased as an influence (except in the negative sense: 'Yes, well, she's like her father in that, I'm afraid').

As a child I just accepted the irrelevance of the Spencer side. It was obvious that we got all our *good* traits from the Steeles— just look at the photo: you would never manage to get the *Spencers* sitting together quietly in a photo like that.

The Spencer side also believed 'education breaks up marriages' and 'you'd be better off leaving and getting a job', but drank and smoked and played cards and didn't go to church so often. The aunties and uncles in this family took time off work and took their kids down to Rosebud every summer holidays and camped in huge tents. They mixed freely with the other campers.

*

Are you allowed to just take the family you want and leave the rest?

My mother is spring-cleaner and caretaker of the family history. She tidies regularly, throwing out the photos that don't fit into the albums, the ones that don't 'look' like their subjects or which are no longer relevant to our 90s version family. (The ex-wives, for instance—kept in a plastic bag in the bottom of her bedroom cupboard.) And so somehow the stern dark Effie has been lost.

Sometimes I rescue the little bits, the bones, the debris, the scattered pieces and cast-offs and take them home, back to Sydney for safe-keeping. I like to sort through them. I don't put my photos in albums, I keep them jumbled together in a big plastic bag. That way every time you take them out a whole new history unfolds, a whole new arrangement and order.

I'm a junk collector. A Steptoe. *(Like your father.)*

In the past year another photo of Effie has turned up. In this one (the *'real'* Effie?) she is dimpled and smiling, coat flapping open and sprinkled with confetti like Santa snow.

The six-white-horse-rider of my dreams.

The two sisters are with her again (permanent attachments?— or perhaps it was the same day, just a different angle). She died a few months later.

Forty-three years ago.

Last year: in a Balwyn lounge room, with my father, his eldest sister and youngest brother, looking at a photo of all the children lined up beside the grave at her funeral. The room goes heavy and quiet. Someone changes the subject before they all start crying.

'Stand up for yourself,' Effie would repeatedly tell my mother when she first married (one farrier's wife to another). 'Don't let him get away with things.'

'I didn't go along with the way she went off at the children,' my mother says. 'But she was really … *lovely.*'

And in fact she may not have been Scottish, after all.

Hugh her husband was the Scottish one, but Effie's father's family were originally from England.

And her mother's family?

*

Another missing photo: the one Aunty May remembers Effie's father showing her one day up at Talbot.

'What do you think of my little mother?' The photo was of a young girl in a cotton gingham dress. She had fair skin, but her features were Koori. ('Like a little native girl,' May remembers.)

'Don't show them that!' her Grandmother Alice (Effie's mother) scolded, taking the photo away. 'Don't go giving the children ideas.'

That photo too has disappeared.

But I think it may have been Maria, Alice's mother (Effie's Grandmother) born in 1852. The S—s were apparently proud, 'very English'. But in the print-out of their family tree someone gave me there are lots of question marks. Great-great-great Grandfather S. came to Melbourne by ship in 1844; but his daughter-in-law, my Great-great Grandmother, is simply 'Maria (?????), born at ??????, died at Amherst, Vic.'

Aunty Jane says when she used to ask as a child why some of them were so dark—an Uncle, for example, was known around Talbot for years as 'Darkie Collins'—the answer was always evasive or vague. 'Indian blood ...' (The gap between Sally Morgan's Perth and our Melbourne maybe not so big after all.)

And then of course there's Neil.

It's my father's 70th birthday party and we have various borrowed photos of his family on display. I show my brother Mike the photo of Neil.

'Who's *that*?' he says in a suspicious voice.

'Well Mike,' I put my arm on his shoulder, 'that's your Uncle Neil.'

He stares at the photo in amazement.

Neil, the wild one. My father's beloved brother who crashed a borrowed motorbike and was killed on his 16th birthday, only a few months after Effie's death.

The one who stopped swimming at the local Balwyn baths because he would get picked on for being so dark. 'Did you see the A— in the pool today?' people would say derogatively and the Spencer kids would realise they were talking about Neil.

'I don't believe it,' Mike says slowly. Then turns and walks away.

His wife says, 'No-ooo.' Then looks again. 'No, a lot of Scottish people were dark like that.'

She'd been telling me earlier how she would like to go back and visit Finland, where she was born and lived until she was ten, but wants Mike to go with her. He refuses and she feels that he can't or won't accept that side of her, that she is Finnish as well as Australian.

'Yes, Scots can be very dark.' She looks again, shakes her head and then backs away, 'Anyway, that's my story and I'm sticking to it!'

Aunty May: 'He used to always stand just a little apart from everyone else, even in all the photos. A loner.'

What would it have been like if he had lived, if he'd been here at the party today?

Mike says he remembers him visiting on the day he was killed. 'He was wild,' he says disapprovingly.

'What sort of wild?'

'Just wild. Like any kid, I guess, but really wild.'

*

In our Steele-identified family, anger (wildness) didn't exist. We were never angry, we never fought.

*

There is always the temptation with the ones you've never met, the ones who died, to think that maybe if they hadn't died, if they'd been there in your childhood, or were still there, things might be different.

But I want the wild Effie, too. The missing one. The angry stern woman. This Effie would *never* whisper wimpishly, 'Let me go (please).' This one, if she needed to, would say, 'Get out of here! Leave me alone!'

Effie is the ghost, the grandmother I might have had.

'She'll be riding six white horses' (the lost photo)

'Watch it!' (The Sisterhood)

*

I wonder sometimes if I'll be kept in the family albums passed down to my nephews and nieces, and if so, which versions of me. Which colour hair? Will they accept the red-headed and black-haired, or only the 'true' brown-haired ones?

Will there be photos of me in my Sydney inner-city houses, ramshackle and filled with bits and pieces of old furniture and artwork, or only ones taken on visits? The photos of me at the weddings, for instance, or sitting in a chair in my mother's clean suburban house.

'That's your weird Aunty Beth,' my brothers used to say to their small puzzled children. 'Now go and give her a kiss.'

NEW SHOES

There is a photo from the mid 1960s I call 'The daggiest family in the world'. It is a snap of my brother and sister and I—the three youngest—and our border-collie farm dog called George, standing out the front of our house in Yarra Glen. Even our house was daggy. A modern house plonked on top of a bare hill.

In another version of this photo we've shoo-ed George off to the side to show off our shoes better. But I like this one (the reject): the downcast modest gaze of us girls. George may have been just a dog, but he was a *male* dog.

In this we are nine (me), eleven and fourteen, wearing, of course, Sunday best. For my brother: black suit, white shirt, white socks, fake folded hanky in his breast pocket and a rather groovy tie (from Coles). For us girls: home-made A-line dresses, white cardigans, ankle socks and the *piece de resistance*, matching white dress shoes with dark blue patent leather toes.

The daggiest family in the world

Outrageous shoes, a children's version of the ones Jean Shrimpton wore at Flemington Racetrack in 1965 and my first attempt at independence, except my sister went and chose the same ones.

We also both have our hair pushed into a stiff 'wave' at the front with a kind of gooey green hair lotion.

We were the mini-family within the larger family. The younger generation. The 1960s family as opposed to the 1950s one. (Beatles, mu-mu dresses—which we always spelt 'moo-moos'—The Monkees, transistor radios, LP records, Barbie dolls.) The post-scarcity family: we had a bedroom each whereas the earlier one lived for many years in a two roomed bungalow.

We were also the first to break a long family tradition and 'stay on at school' past fifteen.

In our family we watched: *Father Knows Best, Andy Griffith, Bachelor Father, My Three Sons, Gomer Pyle USMC, Beverley Hillbillies, Sunny Side Up, The Addams Family, The Munsters, Bewitched, Bandstand, The Jetsons, I Love Lucy,* the *Hardy Family* movies, and *National Velvet.*

If you had any books at all you had enough books, and there were plenty of old Sunday School prizes and Reader's Digests on the shelf. Libraries were unknown: dark dusty places like Catholic Churches. None of us had ever been inside one.

But books were my escape hatch. I fantasised about writing to Louisa M. Alcott until I found out I was eighty years too late. Once I rang Penguin (having seen their sign on a brick fence in Ringwood) and said 'a friend of mine' had written a story and what should she do. The woman said, 'Tell your "friend" to send in her story and we'll have a look.' I didn't though.

I would discover new books (Dr Suess's *Cat in the Hat* or Enid Blyton's *Magic Faraway Tree*) at other people's houses and gobble them up frantically before we had to leave. Or I'd beg to be allowed to borrow my Aunties' Sunday School prize books when my mother's ran out.

I was the quiet one, the knitter, the runt of the litter, the skinny one. The one if she turned sideways would disappear.

My mother says that my headmaster once told her I was a natural leader. She thought he must be confusing me with someone else.

The one at the end of the line can get an unusual amount of freedom because there are just too many things happening and too many others to worry about to keep too close an eye on her.

She spins her black wool while no one is looking. Keeps the ball in her pocket.

School and home; worlds and other-worlds; mine revolved and clashed into each other at night, causing dents and bruises, flashing lights, angry fists raised out of windows, obscene phone calls …

As a teenager I stopped reading because there were no books around, but I recognised education as my ticket out. I won scholarships, I got good marks, I set my sights on university.

My brother went to Swinburne Tech, and then later became a minister; my sister completed fifth form ('what a waste, she'll only get married anyway'), worked for a few years, got married, went back to study and then she too became a minister.

In our family if anyone ever did go to university it was because they were *incredibly* brainy and it was to become a doctor or a teacher. Or in my case, a social worker.

Week one of Sociology 101. My tutor says in a bored voice, 'How many of you want to be social workers?'

Most of us put up our hands.

'Band-aiding the system,' she pronounced. We were horrified. But within a month I'd come to agree with her and changed over to straight Arts.

My mother was right: education does break up families. I moved out of home.

I 'changed'. ('Don't worry, Mum, five out of six isn't bad,' my brothers joke.)

At uni I constructed for myself an alternative family, as different as I could make it—people who liked art and music and literature and left-wing politics and ideas and having a good time (sex and drugs and rock'n'roll)—the grooviest family in the world!

But despite the surface differences, it took me a very long time to realise that I had reproduced in this new one so many of the elements and dynamics of the old. Out of loss and the crucible of childhood, I had recreated for myself another family of big brothers and sisters, taking up my place as little sister, slotting myself in where I felt I belonged, where I felt 'safe'.

(So much harder to leave home than I thought.)

Jenny has groovy shoes too, but this time hers are different

Every family member is a competing family historian.

I make no claims to be objective; I'm right in the thick of my family, knee deep, up to my neck, over my head in some places. And I'm a habitual fiction writer, a rewriter of history. I don't even remember which bits are true any more, and which bits I've made up.

So perhaps this is the time to put in a disclaimer: any resemblance to people living or dead is purely … relative?

This is the view from *my* house—or one of the views. (Have your salt-shaker ready.)

Enter at your own risk.

(Careful, now, Ajax, don't bite the visitors.)

*

I'm the little one, the youngest of six.

I'm the one held down and tickled till she wept for mercy ('But you're laughing, see, you must *like* it').

I'm the little girl laughing, enjoying cuddling her brothers, massaging their bare backs as they lie on the floor in front of the tv in summer, getting them drinks, kissing them on the lips until one of them reaches puberty and says abruptly (and without explaining why) not to do that any more.

And I'm the little girl out on the lawn on hot summer nights, stomping exhaustedly after the tennis ball, whining to be allowed to give up, with my sister dancing off to another corner of the lawn with the tennis racket saying,

'No, don't give up, Becky, you'll get me out this time, I'm *sure* you will'.

*

Faces in the Mob

I'm the little girl, sitting at the table with all the kangaroos. I'm too young to know the rules, the subtle nods and grunts of authority, deference and challenge constantly being passed back and forth between the head kangaroo and his sons.

I'm the smallest, sweet little Beth, Grandma's favourite, *good* little Beth; and I'm the eleven-year-old standing in the garden in front of the flowering noxious weed bush, swearing in a great venomous flood, every filthy vicious word I can think, feeling shame to the roots of my hair but unable to stop. And I'm the little girl terrified her father is going to leave us when he yells at my sister and says 'bloody' and storms out of the house.

He comes back. We say nothing about it.

*

I still love sit-coms. I get a clutching feeling at my stomach when the theme music of the sad and soppy family ones come on. It's like pornography, I try to fight it but it works on me anyway.

*

Xmas Day

I like to stay home alone on Christmas day and work. (ie. I stay home, I don't 'go home'.) I like that secret pocket of free air in between all the family dinner tables around the world as the believers rush about getting there.

I feel naked and a little naughty as I skip about and do what I like. I ride the slip stream of the family tables and let the wind catch my hair. So many headed for disaster (too much alcohol, too much heat, too much roast turkey and plum pudding, too many issues never resolved). I watch them roar past.

*

I have no family; and I have this huge enormous one; and I have lots of families.

*

Magic Shoes

One Saturday I was standing by the car in the main street of Lilydale waiting for my mother, minding my own business, when two girls about my own age walked past.

'Look!' yelled one of them rudely, pointing at my feet. 'Her toes are blue! She's got a disease!' And they laughed and laughed all the way down the street.

Of course my shoes were ruined after that. But somehow despite their delicate precarious and now-injured flamboyance, they remained the sturdiest most durable and perfectly fitting shoes in history. I had to wear them for years.

How could something that easily destroyed be so unbreakable?

THE MORE THINGS CHANGE

The mid 60s: In the evenings my brother takes the farm dogs out into the paddock and swings them round by their tails. My sister and I scream, 'Stop it, you're hurting them!' He hurls them off into the air. 'Look, they love it,' he says, and they run back for more, leaping and snapping their teeth, tongues lolling.

The smell of milk and oil and manure and superphosphate and rust.

Inside, on hot afternoons, the click of the billiard balls on green felt. I walk around collecting the red balls out of the pockets like eggs, putting them into a small round cane basket.

In the boys' room there is a bed in each corner and a billiard table in the middle. Dusty brown and green chenille bedspreads. A geometric design curtain hides the guns hanging on the wall beside Mike's bed.

When I was two, he would take me out on the tractor while he unloaded hay for the cows and let me drive. I'd yell out, 'Mike, Mike, tree!' or 'Mike, fence!' and he'd leap over the back and take the wheel until it was all clear again. He built a blackboard for me on the wall of the back room when I was four, under the line of washing, next to the purple wooden box for the gumboots. In the morning the others would write words or sums on it before they went to school and I'd disappear inside it for hours.

I don't recall him ever using my name. In a crowded room he'll just say, 'Hey, love', and I'll turn to him. My sister is the same. Like there are wires attaching us to him.

He is the invader of my dreams, with his guns and axes, his competence and endurance and strength, his certainty of right.

He can make me cry with some of his comments. 'Please don't use that word, Mike.'

His voice is soft, he never has to raise it. Even for the punch-line. 'You call them that because that's the sound they make when you hit 'em with a ute.'

I hop in my car and drive like a maniac till I reach the border, only stopping when I am over the bridge at Tocumwal.

I eat my lunch on the NSW bank, watching the river.

The Old Man

The New Man?

At the end of 60s I tunnelled my way through the blackboard, down under the foundations of the house, past the base of the brick chimney where my sister kept her science experiments, past the rags and stuffing of my little toy rabbit left behind one winter and eaten by the mice, out into the paddocks and down the road to the 70s.

The 70s man used K.O. hairspray instead of Brylcreem (even my father, eventually), and exchanged his white shirts for pink ones (or blue or green).

Our move to the suburbs marked the end of the battle of the kangaroos; each of my eldest brothers now had a farm of his own. But Old George and Young George (we tended to lack imagination when it came to naming dogs)—brought in from two different farms to retire in peace—battled it out in the backyard ferociously until we sent Old George back.

Then I tunnelled my way to uni, and eventually I packed my bags and fled to Sydney. I have New Men friends, with the smell of baby-sick on their shirts as they discuss their current work projects and give me love and support for mine.

But sometimes I feel as though just my head has got free and my shoulders are stuck in the tunnel. I still get my head turned by working-class bad boys: tall silent risk-takers. Soft speakers who say 'love' and all the little wires plugged into my body jump as they offer me a ride on the back of their motorbikes or in their fast cars.

I want to go back inside that tunnel and come out again, start over, all fresh and bloody and get washed down and cradled by strong hands that smell of baby powder rather than gun grease.

I'm tired of cosmetic changes and I want 'real' ones. But I'm not even sure what that means any more.

*

In our 70s family we watched *MacMillan and Wife, Columbo, Countdown, All in the Family, The Restless Years, Days of Our Lives, The Partridge Family, The Brady Bunch, Poseidon Adventure* and *Charlies Angels*. And in later years, when I was the only one left at home, I would pull the comfortable chair close to the tv after my parents went to bed, eat cakes brought home from the Milk Bar where I worked, and watch *Radio with Pictures, Monty Python*, and repeats of *Four Corners*. And once, very very late, Ingmar Bergman's *The Virgin Spring* which freaked me out totally.

*

And where was Ajax? Left behind under the house at Yarra Glen. Fretting and stamping his feet. 'I will never forget you,

Ajax!' I cried silently to myself as we followed the removals truck out the driveway.

But of course I did.

*

What's in a name?

Hteb /he-teb/, *n.:* (Martian—semi-obsolete) small carved wooden bowl which the woman takes, fills with clear spring water, kneels and presents to the man when he returns from the hunt or from war. The ceremony of the hteb bowl …

MEETINGS OF GREAT MINDS …

On the back of this photo it says, *'Chip—5 yrs 7 mths. Beth—7 mths.'* Which means it was still in that innocent time when he believed I was his because he'd been told, before I was born, that he might get a little brother or sister for his birthday.

The two Scorpios; ratbags, lefties, mad ones. Our friendship was strongest in the years when I was twelve to fifteen and he was seventeen to twenty; when he started bringing home student newspapers from Swinburne Tech and we discovered a common interest in politics. There were threats to separate us at the dinner table because we cracked jokes no one else could understand and talked so much. And when he broke his collar bone and I'd go into his room late at night to talk and muck about and help him change into his pyjama top, my mother would hover uneasily around the door. ('Beth, isn't it past your bedtime?')

He joined the ministry; we added theology, history and philosophy to our discussions. He spent his weekdays at the College.

'Now Chip's coming home this weekend and he's very busy so you *mustn't disturb him,*' my mother would warn. The weekends were for spending with his fiancé.

'Tell him that, not me,' I'd mutter, but who would believe an eighteen-year-old might actually seek out his thirteen-year-old sister's company. It's so natural for a girl to look up to a boy, especially her big brother. Puppy love, hero worship, she has a crush on her brother—I knew what they were thinking.

Sometimes he'd come in and wake me at two a.m. to tell me that he and his fiancé had split up, and then ask me to break the news to Mum. A week or two later he'd be back with her again and we'd say nothing about it.

If I had been a little older (a little more experienced). But I wasn't. I listened, I did what he asked. I kept my misgivings to myself. Years later he said, if only someone had said something … But what could I do?

*

Little sister-big brother can be a special bond because in some ways she is a younger, more companionable version of mother. Good at providing nurture (well-trained), and if she's the youngest she'll comply with almost anything just to be taken along. A little (m)other. A highly polished mirror. A pocket version.

But in fact this was a time of deep rift between my mother and me. I had begun wearing my black wool (faded jeans, torn sneakers), staying in my room at night to study, hanging out with boys (but not boyfriends) and discussing un-girl things. And even though I alternated this with periods of high-femininity (dresses, make-up, neatly crossed legs), I didn't have a Boyfriend, which as the years wore on, began to strike fear into my mother's heart.

When I was nine I was getting dressed one morning when I overheard my mother and one of my brothers talking in the kitchen and I raced out to disagree with him. 'The sheep's paddock is *full* of deadly night shade and the sheep are *eating it!*' My brother didn't say anything, he just looked at me. I followed his gaze and realised I'd rushed out wearing only my petticoat. I blushed and ran back to my room.

Adolescence was a bit like that.

'A bikini,' Chip said one day, stopping in his tracks as he met me walking along the camping ground track. 'Does Mum know you've got that on?'

Another time: walking the length of the shopping centre car park after work to get to where he and his fiancé were waiting for me. I had on my white mini uniform, platform shoes, tan stockings. I had a red rinse in my hair for the first time. When I got in the back seat he switched on the ignition and said calmly, 'I never realised how stumpy your legs were'.

He said it like it was a comment on the colour of the automatic doors or the size of the pet-shop sign. His fiancé told him off (crossing her long slender legs and pulling her skirt down an inch), but I felt like it was a test; I was supposed to just take it. I was above things like that, wasn't I?

(Don't feel it. Don't notice.)

*

I had this troublesome female body. But I kind of liked it too, I liked dressing it up, taking it out with me …

*

At sixteen I wiggled out of that frying pan, swan-diving into another. David was also older (better educated, more knowledgeable). We wrote ten page letters three or four times a week. Hour long phone calls.

It was 'platonic' in the sense that he went to great pains to make clear in his first letter that I mustn't harbour any false 'hopes'. He had *lots* of girl *friends*. And then he proceeded to flirt with me, erratically, in private and public, for the next two years.

We had another, mutual, male friend to whom I was also writing, and after a year I received a typed and photocopied letter with the mysterious initials F.S.G.P.E. after my name. The letter announced that I'd been nominated to become a fellow of 'The Society for the Greatest People on Earth'. I was flattered—who wouldn't be? In its entire history I was the first female *ever* to be offered membership.

*

I'm seventeen; on a camping trip to which David has invited me with his older, more educated and sophisticated friends.

One morning he comes in to the girls' tent and does some romping and teasing while we are still in our sleeping bags; that is, he does it with everyone except me. I know I don't look my best in the mornings (or on camping trips with no showers or mirrors), but I try not to worry about it. David says conversationally, 'I could never marry anyone who looked terrible in the morning.'

(Don't feel it. Don't notice …)

*

The rules are slippery. Society hands the man a pack that's been stacked, and you can feel everyone sitting around watching to see how you're going to cope.

*

(Was it really so impossible to think a girl might be interested in a boy just for his brains?)

*

I took the option of becoming totally passive. Desireless; making myself, or pretending to be, asexual. To react to the flirting and innuendos would have been somehow fatal. It would risk expulsion from the club. And 'I don't want *you* for a boyfriend' might have made my loyalty suspect. 'I don't want *any* boyfriend' was much safer.

Safer for me to believe too. It protected both of us.

So what's left when you can't be a buddy or a mate because you're too obviously female (and when the female bit is obviously part of the package that interests them)? And when you're too whatever—smart, challenging, unpredictable?—to be girlfriend material?

The little sister role. A perfect solution because it was one with which we were both familiar. It gave me a certain freedom to move about with the boys and even be quite close (a special bond). And it enabled the man to control it.

*

This time I'm fifteen: my brother and I are standing in a group of his friends (our friends?) and suddenly he peers at me and says, 'You've got make-up on!' There is an awkward silence. No one knows what to say. I blush.

Listen. Hear that whirring sound? It's the little-sister security grille lowering into place, locking us into position. Entwined, tugged close, collapsed against his chest, held possessively tight, head wedged firmly under his chin. (Better not to move at all, be grateful to be held, if you wiggle too much you might get dropped.)

This was a structure that fitted neatly over several new relationships in the following years, until I realised that although it acted as a special passport to intimacy, the costs were more than I was willing to pay. And the feeling of security was an illusion.

*

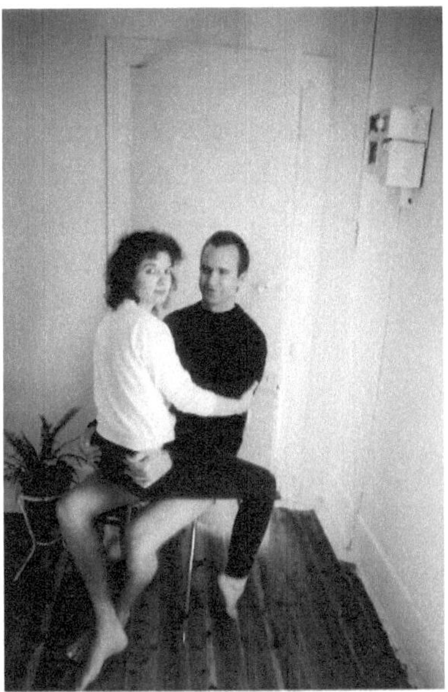

I'm a big girl now

I stay on my toes. I keep the door open. I leave when it's no longer comfortable …

Well, at least that's the fantasy …

Here's another: If I was the *eldest* (instead of the youngest) …

*

The original family is like a puzzle in a dream that one hasn't quite 'got'. You keep repeating the dream so you can keep going over and over it.

You can get trapped in the recurring nightmare—backed into a corner, where your only option is to keep hurting each other. Or perhaps you can use the dream to examine your life and find a way out.

*

My father: reaching into his pocket for something while we are in the bank together and then offering me the copper coins. 'Dad, I'm 35. I don't want your two cent pieces!' He looks surprised a moment, blushes and puts them back.

*

What's in a name? 2

There's an episode on *Get Smart* where the model, Miss Spencer, gets sprayed with a hardening agent by Kaos and turned into a plastic mannequin. Max Smart is in the steam room with all the mannequins trying to get them to revive. One of the dummy's arms falls off in Max's hand, 'A bit late for you I'm afraid, fella.'

*

I came into my office for something last night and saw the photo of me as a baby sitting on my brother's knee. And I thought: that little baby broke my parents' marriage. I hate her.

*

When you are the straw that broke the camel's back you carry a burden of guilt, a legacy of grief …

*

No one sits still anymore. We have become restless with the old poses. My mother at seventy-two picks the lock on her wedding ring with just a thin wire held between her teeth. My father spins around, threatening to disappear.

Memory plays tricks, but that's why I like it. A kind of magic. Like photographs, capturing things, holding them up to the light long enough for you to see the patterns. Like writing, or therapy.

I've decided to shut my eyes. I like the blackness. I can feel my way along the walls to the space between the two doors; there is a small door handle in my palm that I fit into a tiny hole. I write myself into the family, in order to write myself out of it. I am the family escape artist. (I can provide lessons.)

I have knocked on the boards for a long time and have found the stone rooms in between the skirting boards, and the people who are glad to see me and who love me for who I am. It's not perfect (it smells of toast and damp socks, after all). We smash the china sometimes and occasionally rip up the velvet dresses in our fury at each other, but this is my home now. This is where I feel safe.

My mother comes and visits now and then. I send messages and postcards back along the tunnel to the rest of the family. And when I want to, I can lock the door. I can say the magic words and the cracks will seal up. I can dance and twirl in my blue-toed shoes. And I can hear them searching and searching, their socks scuffing softly on the shiny floor.

Yesterday I had a few friends drop by …

Many people say that fiction is just a bunch of lies.
I would say that fiction is the best way of finding truth.
—Amy Tan

Notes and Acknowledgements

A note on 'The True Story of an Escape Artist':

Back when I wrote this piece there were questions raised in our family that perhaps we had First Nation ancestors on my father's side. But in the past year I've had the chance to look more closely into the family history with the aid of records uploaded to Ancestry.com and have seen documents that show that all my ancestors arrived here by boat in the nineteenth century. There are, it turns out, a number of other deeply buried secrets in the family, but this was not one of them.

*

An early version of **Bewitching** was published as 'Samantha – Every Witch Way But Lose' in *The Age*, with a more recent version in *Burrow* and in the Poetry at the Pub anthology, *Take Heart.*

Fatal Attraction in Newtown was first published in *Picador New Writing 2*, ed Helen Daniel and Drusilla Modjeska; then in *How to Conceive of a Girl* (Random House, 1996). I've included it here on the thirty-fifth anniversary of the film as, unfortunately, it seems as relevant as ever, with the #MeToo movement and an increasing recognition of how violence against women can so easily be made to seem 'normal' in our culture.

The Age of Fibs is adapted from a section of 'A Short (personal) History of the Bra and its Contents' which was the creative component of my PhD thesis, *The Body as Fiction / Fiction as a way of Thinking* (University of Ballarat). Parts of this story also prefaced an essay called 'Bras, Breasts and Living in the Seventies: Historiography in the Age of Fibs', in *Australian Feminist Studies: Seventies Issue*.

The Angel of the Forest Has a Migraine was inspired by Allana Beltran, the Weld Forest Angel, with thanks to all forest protectors. It was first published in *Plumwood Mountain: a journal of eco poetry*.

Playing the Man: Memories of Football was originally commissioned by Claudia Taranto and broadcast on ABC Radio National's *In the Mix*. Also published in *Ulitarra*, in *The Age*, and reprinted in *Storyweavers* (Macmillan Educational), edited by Sandra Bernhardt.

Ex-centric was originally published as a poem in *The Australian*.

Playing Cards on a Red Rattler was first published in *Mascara*, 'Class Fetish' issue.

Ready, Willing appeared in *Live Encounters 12th Anniversary edition*.

The Mummy's Foot won *The Age* Short Story Award and was published in *The Age*, and then as a 'prose poem' in *Things in a Glass Box* (Five Island Press New Poets Series). An audio version was produced as part of a program based on *Things in a Glass Box* for ABC-RN's *Poetica*. Text in italics in this story is inspired by and adapted from Mildred Place, *Wrapped for Eternity* (1977).

A version of **White Noise** was published in *The Canberra Times*.

Two Stories on a Train was first published in *The Phoenix Review*, and then in *How to Conceive of a Girl*.

Benefits was a finalist in the joanne burns microlit awards and published in *Pulped Fiction* (Spineless Wonders).

Dance, with Red Wool – an earlier version was published in *LinQ*.

***The Littlest Hobo* Travels *Adventure Island* and Waiting for Rain** are from *Vagabondage* (UWAP, 2014).

By My Look's Caress began as a performance piece using four sources—a story of mine, a romance novel I found in an Op Shop, a 1950s dating manual, and an essay by film theorist Christian Metz. It was written for *Putting on an Act*, a week of performances organised by the Artworkers Union and was later published in *My Look's Caress: a collection of modern romances*, ed. Beth Yahp, Margot Daly and Lorraine Falconer (Local Consumption). It was also produced as part of a feature on category romance for ABC-RN's *In the Mix*.

Blade was a finalist in the joanne burns microlit awards and published in *Shuffle: microlit anthology* (Spineless Wonders).

Doing the Rock was first published in *Westerly*, and later in *Gangway* magazine. It was produced as a sound piece for ABC-FM's *The Listening Room* by Claudia Taranto. The *TerraRock* photographs are by Helen Kundicevic from her series exhibited at The Tin Sheds in Sydney and reproduced in the book *TerraRock* with text by Simon Enticknap (Sydney: Deadreal).

Since You was first published in *Grieve*. This one is for my brother Geoff, in memory of his much-loved wife Carita (10-6-1948 – 25-11-2012).

A version of **Forgetting** was published in *Vagabondage*, and was performed for Radio National's *Earshot*. This piece is in memory of my mother Iris Vera Florence Spencer (1.8.1921—27.8.2017).

When You Hold Me (The Bra Monologues) was first published in *Best Australian Stories*, edited by Robert Drew and in *The Party of Life* (Flying Islands).

'The True Story of an Escape Artist' was written for the collection *Family Pictures*, commissioned and edited by Beth Yahp (HarperCollins), with an extract broadcast on ABC-RN's *Radio Eye*.

Tracking Back, A Dispatch from Cheryl in the Museum of Desire, Daydream Believing, Rising and Falling, Extinction Event, After, Time, In the Hologram Forest, On Turning Sixty and After Shingles, and **The Death of Mr Propinquity** are all published here for the first time.

Audio versions of some of these pieces can be found on the double CD *Body of Words* (Dogmedia, 2004), and at my YouTube and Soundcloud channels, which are linked from my website at www.bethspencer.com. Other resources for teachers and students are also available at this website, including a link to a YouTube playlist of video 'footnotes'.

*

My heartfelt thanks to all the many editors and radio producers who commissioned, published and/or encouraged me through writing some of these pieces, especially Claudia Taranto and Beth Yahp; to my very patient PhD supervisors Meg Tasker and Fiona Giles; to Carmel Bird for her lifetime of inspiring creativity and for supporting and judging the Carmel Bird Digital Literary Award in 2018; to Sophie Amos for being a wonderful and dedicated intern and for all she did to help get this book on the road; to brilliant typesetter Camilla Cripps; to the amazing Spineless Wonders publisher and editor Bronwyn Mehan for her tireless work and creativity finding ways to get unusual stories and books out into the world; and to all those writers, editors, publishers, broadcasters, reviewers and readers who participate in and contribute to creative cultures in Australia and beyond.

My great thanks to the Literature Board of the Australia Council for fellowships in the past; to CreateNSW for a 'quick response' grant in December 2021 to complete this book; and to Varuna Writers Centre for setting up a daily zoom 'writing room' during the pandemic and to the wonderful writers I met and silently worked alongside as we connected across the distance, and the chats we had before and after.

Thank you to Helen Kundicevic for friendship and for the use of her beautiful 'TerraRock' photos and the reconstructed photos in 'The True Story of an Escape Artist'.

Thanks also to friends who participated in the reconstructions—Helen Kundicevic and Christina Spurgeon in 'The Sisterhood'; Jenny Hocking and Daryl Dellora (and unknown cat) in 'New Shoes'; Bruce Gregory in 'I'm a Big Girl Now'; Ian Wansbrough as 'The New Man?'; and in the last photo—the family of creation—the participants are (*from left to right: back row*) Daphne Andersen, Margaret Coombs, Phillip Briant, Raphael Briant, Me, Ian Wansbrough, Henry Andersen, Claudia Taranto, Christina Spurgeon, Lucy Thompson, Stephen Thompson, Michael Perdices, (*front row*) Anne Delaney, Tricia McCormick, Andrea Collison, Simon Enticknap, Anne Melano, Ludmila Fields, Deborah George, and Paul Fitzgerald.

It always moves me to look at this photograph and know that those babies are now interesting young adults, and that two of my friend-family departed way too young: in memoriam, Deborah George and Margaret Coombs. Some I have lost contact with; others—while older, greyer and wiser—are still beloved friends.

Thank you also to family members for allowing the use of the original photographs; to my brother Brian Spencer; and to Phillip Oldfield, a wonderfully compassionate and skilled Gestalt therapist who first showed me how to open the door and find a way out of the woods.

Loving gratitude to my writing group for many years—Peta Spear, Catherine Moffatt and Jennifer Kremmer; to Jenny Hocking, Daryl Dellora, Anita Hoare and Sarah Minife for decades of friendship and for reading and commenting on work; and to the many friends (old and new, and including those I have only met virtually) who have kept me going with their love and encouragement for what I do. Such friendships are priceless.

And finally—thank you as always Ian Wansbrough for being such a strong and intelligent reader, editor and supporter of my work. Thank you for so many great conversations, and for helping to make writing fun.

This work has been produced while living in what is called NSW and Victoria on Aboriginal land that has never been ceded. I would like to acknowledge the Traditional Owners and pay my respects to Elders past and present. Always was, always will be. Thank you for your continuing connection to and care for land and waters, and community. May a Treaty and restorative justice become a priority in these lands.

May there always be art, and friendship, as we move into this time of unimaginable climate crisis.

May there always be hope.

www.bethspencer.com

ES-PRESS

www.shortaustralianstories.com.au/es-press